A SIMPLE REBELLION

By
CHRISTOPHER RYAN

A SEAMUS AND NUNZIO PRODUCTIONS BOOK

A SIMPLE REBELLION

Political Horror
Published by Seamus and Nunzio Productions, LLC
508 Windsor Rd., New Milford, NJ 07646

Follow the author at:
Facebook/Christopher Ryan, Author
Twitter @chrisryanwrites
Instagram @chrisryanwrites
chrisryanwrites@wordpress.com

ISBN: 978 – 1981802395

Cover and interior design by Tonia Andrews

First print edition, January, 2018

First ebook edition, January, 2018

In a future uncomfortably close to our present....

Chapter 1

CALIFORNIA WAS FIRST. IT happened less than 48 hours after the president announced his intention to run for a third term, damn the 22nd Amendment. On every platform across the Internet the state's governor posted, "We're done," and attached articles of cessation.

California fast became the eighth most robust economy on the planet, so good on them, but Bob Murphy missed thinking of his native country as the *United* States of America.

Now it was just The States, fractured into pieces. Some were plunged into devastating poverty. Others saw their economy driven into the ground by the one percent of the one percent of the one percent, the rest of its citizens suffering under a greatly reduced standard of living. The areas still clutching former glory were speeding toward economic depression through deficit spending and denial.

No matter where they subsisted, workers were treated as slaves; job security, pensions, and health benefits were myths from the past. The states in each region served as neo-feudal colonies, with pestilent living conditions ignored by National News.

That last term bears repeating.

National News.

This was the name of the sole remaining FCC-licensed 24-hour news station, fully funded and run by the government. That was another gift from *him*.

Correction, *president him*.

Bob knew capitalization was supposed to come into play, but he just couldn't do it, not even in his thoughts.

That breach of protocol would catch up to him, he acknowledged.

Everything eventually did these days.

God bless America.

The teenager, a tall, gangly kid sporting a poorly self-made Mohawk and a chip on his shoulder the size of Detroit, dominated the dashboard, repeatedly reaching forward between Bob and his adult son, Jackson, demanding more from the struggling air conditioning, blasting what he insisted was music, demanding Bob appreciate the musicians' genius even after he identified them as Mute Nostril Agony.

They sounded like a metal band from Bob's era doing an acoustic set; lots of lightening fast riffs played really softly as if even head bangers were afraid to draw too much attention to themselves in this era of swift enforcement for perceived offenses.

> *Well fed sons of middle class mothers,*
> *Wander lost in their father's dreams, ruined*

Welcome to the party, boys

Bob was driving west on the straight highway that used to plow through Pennsylvania farm country. Now the fields were gray and fallow, long stretches torn up by fracking, fields barren like the crops had just given up. The benefit was he could see anyone coming for miles. The problem was, if another car did appear where would he go to avoid being seen? The best he could hope for was a dirt road turnoff appearing at the right time.

Bob didn't like his odds on that.

His son, Jackson, the dog, and the little girl all slept soundly, the teenager buried himself in the music, and Bob drove, keeping an eye out for any upcoming exit that would return them to the even more deserted back roads offering less chance of capture.

He drove through the night with his headlights off, and argued with himself over his culpability in all of this.

Most people were heading to Washington, D.C. because of him. He felt guilty but it wasn't his fault, not really.

Bob sighed. Of course it was his fault. Sheriff Merle was the teenager and the little girl's father; he should have been protecting them, not some former comedian. That put his demise on Bob. And all the other deaths were on his head, too. Every life lost since he'd opened his wiseass mouth was on him.

And whatever happened to all those people who had listened to him, had followed him into something even he didn't know he had started, their fates would be on him as well.

Why were they all going to D.C. anyway? The overlords had abandoned it long ago. Now the nation's "capital" was exclusively the turf of the lucrative protest industry. Companies charged significant fees to outraged citizens, naïve in their sincerity but willing to pay for the privilege of riding the Resistance Express. Those buses brought loads of law-abiding protestors to the capital so they could march and shout and hold signs and feel they were fighting the good fight for the betterment of their beloved and beleaguered nation.

It was always recorded for the amusement of those in charge ... and so that TASE (the president's True American Safety Enforcement agency) could run facial recognition programs. The latter generated lists of those to be harassed, partly to stoke fear, partly to create the sense that the resistance was making a difference. This generated more business for the bus companies, which, of course, were owned by the very same people the resistance was resisting.

Everybody wins.

Meanwhile, Witchita, Kansas was now the real capital of The United States of True America (TUSOTA), a territory where the murderously rich pulled the strings to create the world they wanted to profit from with almost no recognition of the general populace.

Real power appears as but a shadow of a shadow and likes it that way.

Witchita's primary performance puppet, the president, coined the term "True Americans" to get citizens of TUSOTA to "show loyalty and patriotism" even though its economy was the weakest on the continent. Those who didn't show loyalty (a term that was defined differently from day to day by president him) became "the enemies of True America" and their hunt and capture was broadcast on the highest rated show on television, *Patriotism Live*, which was a primary source of capital for the TUSOTA government.

That damned show had become another source of guilt. Bob had often found himself pitying the poor suckers who were so bad at playing along with the way things were that they wound up with an entire country turned against them. Now Bob, his son, the kid, the sweet little girl, and even the damned dog were featured targets on *Patriotism Live* as "the biggest threat to freedom this nation has ever faced!"

Of course, every target of the show was described the same way, but that did not help Bob relax as he drove through the black gloom toward an exit he couldn't see.

Chapter 2

WHEN THE END BEGAN, Bob Murphy thought he was still stuck in the middle....

A mutated bicycle rolled through the last solitary moments of a suburban night, old supermarket shopping wagons lashed to each side of the rear wheel and laden with bulging plastic bags. On the center of the handlebars sat a padded basket featuring a tiny seatbelt designed to look like a bandoleer. That bandoleer secured a small Yorkie, his fur blowing in the light breeze.

Bob Murphy, an older man, hair mostly gray now, glanced with sharp, saddened eyes at the tiny dog and allowed himself a signature wry smile that had once thrilled many millions around the globe. But instead of making the planet echo with laughter, this mismatched pair coasted silently down the tree-lined street in the pleasant predawn darkness. They glided through town, passing picturesque homes embracing sleeping families, aging cars in the driveway, an occasional old tire hanging idle below a thick tree limb.

Bob whispered, "Pretty nice like this, doncha think?"

The yorkie responded, "Yip."

All else on the streets was quiet. It was the best time for a former comedy icon to move through his community without causing a fuss.

Bob rode to town before the sun came up almost every morning, as he had with Mary Angeline for years. He wore a faded and frayed Bears hoodie and battered Cubs hat as he pedaled through his daily errands, just as he had with Mary Angeline.

Just him and the dog these days, Bob was reminded for the thousandth time that morning. His smile inverted.

He preferred to get going early, before people were on their way to work, before kids were heading to school, before crowds were possible, not wanting to disrupt their lives. The quiet time from 4 to 6 a.m. was his sweet spot.

Mary Angeline had burdened his co-pilot with the name Sasha but Bob usually called him Steve.

But not during their bike rides.

The tiny dog wiggled in his bandoleer seatbelt and yipped again.

"Okay, okay! I'm gonna make the jump to light speed," the comedian answered. "Chewie, angle the deflector shields!"

Bob put his legs into it, picking up the pace, the dog leaning into the stronger breeze. Seeing Steve's enjoyment, Bob pushed himself to go faster.

They rode two miles to the dump. Budget cuts had ended sanitation pick-up two years ago, so those supermarket wagons bracketing his rear tires carried their refuse from the last few days. He tossed the garbage into the large bin outside the dump's front gate.

"Hey, Mac," Bob said, nodding his chin toward the Keeper of the Crap.

"Hey, Bob."

Steve growled a tiny threat.

"You're risking life and limb, Mac. My friend here had fifteen confirmed kills as a Navy SEAL."

Bob left Mac laughing, as usual, and rode back about a mile to their next errand, visiting Pop at his store.

Pop's Country Emporium offered three short, low aisles of food staples, a handful of refrigeration units half full with milk and butter and, sometimes, soda. The front of the store featured an aging luncheonette counter with stools, a few of which still spun a bit. Pop held court there, fixing up sandwiches and grilling meals including a classic burger when there was beef, all served with a smile and easy, safe small talk.

Mary Angeline had taken Bob there on one of their first morning rides. Maybe that explained Bob's loyalty to the place. These days, he ordered most of his supplies from the old couple, everything from groceries to light bulbs to fertilizer to beer.

"Morning, Pop!"

"Hey, Mr. Big Stuff, your order came in," Pop said with a smile, pouring Bob a cup of coffee and then tossing Steve a doggie treat.

Bob saw that the owner already had two eggs and three strips of turkey bacon on the grill. Not as good as real bacon, but all pork had become a delicacy five years ago.

Pop raised a bushy white eyebrow. "What're we toasting today? Rye? Wheat?"

"English?"

"With peanut butter?"

"Peanut butter came in?" Bob broke into a smile. "Who's better than you?"

"Sadly, nobody," the storeowner smiled back, his eyes disappearing amid deep crow's feet.

As Pop prepared Bob's breakfast, the TV mounted in the corner played National News. Finishing the five-day forecast, the Weather Guy announced in his consistently friendly tone, "And remember, it's National Overtime Appreciation Day. If you've been trusted to work a little longer, a bit later, maybe a weekend, today we acknowledge that we're all in this together. Remember to thank your boss for the privilege of working as a True American. And, if you get OT, well, then, today a gift for your boss is appropriate."

Bob watched as the program switched to an impossibly coiffed former jock turned news anchor who spoke meaningfully into the camera. "Fighting continues in the Middle East, with approximately seven neighboring countries battling each other incessantly since the withdrawal of all True American troops..."

Pop placed the fake bacon and eggs in front of Bob, with a toasted English muffin covered with a modest spread of peanut butter, saying quietly, "The world has been spinning out of control since Statler pulled our troops out of, well, everywheres."

Bob dug into the food. "Haven't been following."

Pop topped off his coffee. "Haven't been following, what, the world?"

Bob used chewing to avoid answering. He shrugged, glanced back at the screen.

The anchor continued as, on his left, the screen showed a broad shouldered man with dashing gray hair and sun-bronzed, mature good looks. "The only response from the White House has been President Statler's tweet."

The screen switched to the familiar social media format. The same good looks smiled out from a headshot in the top left corner. The rest of the screen was dominated by the quote.

> @RealPresidentStatler: Sad to see such carnage, but, frankly, this wouldn't have happened if they had paid their fair share for our troops.

Pop tossed Steve another treat, murmuring while barely moving his lips. "Middle East is eating itself and this guy wants to get paid."

Bob's mumbled response was a noncommittal, "Yeah." He drank more coffee and looked around. "Where's Eleanor?"

If Pop recognized the strategic subject change he didn't show it. "She's across town spoiling our new granddaughter."

Bob paused, a forkful of fake bacon in mid-air. "Pictures, please."

From his phone, Pop projected a clip of a chubby infant wriggling in a crib.

Bob's delight was genuine. "Look at her! Those eyes! She's adorable," He offered that trademark smirk, "Can't blame Eleanor for leaving your wrinkled ass."

"Neither can I," Pop chuckled. "If there was more than one store still open in this town I woulda taken the day myself."

They spent the remainder of breakfast focusing on a new local beauty instead of horrors abroad.

Chapter 3

AN ADULT WITH A kid's face and vulture's eyes confronted Bob on his way out of Pop's store with four bags of groceries. Late 20s, Ivy League grad, wearing the current version of a power suit, battleship gray, tailored too tight like they did back in the 'teens, open-collared shirt worn exactly the way *StyledMan* told him to, a throwback, high-end wristwatch wrapped around the same hand used to grasp the iPhone24, a thumb prodding it incessantly.

Bob nudged by him, edging the corporate minion away from his bike and into the gutter. He placed the supplies into the baskets, speaking without looking at the intruder. "Jeremy, we spoke about this."

The guy was all viper smile and insincere cheer. "Bob! You haven't been answering my calls, Bob."

The former comedy star secured Steve into his bandoleer barely glancing the suit's way. "In fact, I have."

"Bob, burping and hanging up immediately does not qualify as communication, bro."

"Seems eloquent to me."

Jeremy shook his head at the bike. "Bob, if you need a car, I can hook you up with anything you want, buddy."

"I own five cars, but in the morning, Steve and I

prefer this mode of travel, thank you very much."

"The mutt carries weight in your decision making? I should've brought that little mop top some bacon."

Bob waved away the bribe of delicacies and sneered, "You trying to kill him?"

Jeremy made a confused face and then hopped back onto the sidewalk, choosing to drop the subject of bacon in favor of taking another approach. "The 30th anniversary of *Monster Cops* is coming up."

Climbing onto the bike, Bob glanced at the young executive with disdain. "Yep."

"We have a massive anniversary edition Blu-Ray coming out."

"Why?"

"To celebrate a comedy classic!"

Bob scoffed, "More like conning fans who can't afford it to buy the same damn again." He shook his head, pushed off, and started pedaling away.

Jogging backward keeping pace with practiced cool, Jeremy pressed his case. "This edition has over 20 hours of essentially never-seen-before footage and behind-the-scenes extras!"

"Essentially," Bob sneered, pedaling a little faster.

Jeremy ran alongside him, twisting forward awkwardly, eyes on his target. "I booked you on *The Tonight Show, Late Night, The Daily Show, and Miller Time.*"

"Booking me without permission is one of your problems."

"One? What's the oth—WHOOFF!" The breath slammed out of Jeremy as he ran into a parking meter. The ancient machine dropped the executive to his knees with minimal effort.

"Bye, Jeremy," Bob called pleasantly as he pedaled off into the morning sun.

Chapter 4

BOB PUT THE GROCERIES and supplies away exactly how Mary Angeline preferred them, the yorkie following him as he crisscrossed the kitchen. "Steve, why did we buy light bulbs again?"

Having no idea, Steve made no comment on the issue.

"Thanks for the insight," Bob quipped.

The supplies stored away, the former favorite of millions wandered into the living room and sat on the aging, once elegant couch. Steve hopped up next to him. Bob worked his battered, duct-taped remote controls, turning on a large-screen television and cable box, clicked open the DVR listings, and selected the latest illegal recording of *The Amy Brooks Update*, already partially watched. As the young Ms. Brooks espoused independent thought, she was not on National News station, and therefore, technically banned. The sheriff's kid had tampered with the cable box – a process he called "jailbreaking" – allowing Bob to view pirate stations the Feds had been unable to track down. Was recording even one episode a federal offense? Sure, but that's life on the edge, Bob mocked himself.

Amy appeared onscreen, jet black hair with a streak of white at the left temple. Bob never found out whether that was from some shock or merely an affectation, but it worked for Amy Brooks. Onscreen, her sharp features leaned forward intently as usual, bright blue eyes crackling with intelligence, small mouth almost always pulled slightly to the right in a smartass smirk even while forming the direst of words. Also as usual, she was elaborately explaining background information designed to underscore her main point. Amy Brooks would set up the imminent arrival of an apocalypse with extensive historical context.

"... each of them presented their own challenges to the American public. Kennedy. Johnson. Nixon. Ford. Carter. Reagan. Bush I. Clinton. Bush II. Obama. Trump. Pence. Ritchie. Each pushed us a little further down the road to the government we now find ourselves living under. Democrat and Republican, Conservative and Liberal, each added to what we are today. Each was complicit, as are we all. We cannot ignore that we all contributed to forming our current government.

"Our ongoing mistake was that we merely survived the calamities of these presidencies; we weathered the changes and betrayals and tightening of our freedoms and liberties, and we each must live with choosing to ignore the dark clouds as they gathered. Now we must ask whether we can endure the perfect storm that is President Beauregard "Bo" Statler."

A picture appeared onscreen behind and to the right of Amy; that of the same broad shouldered, jock-handsome man from the news report Bob watched at Pop's. The square jaw underscored a smile that had been described as either reassuring or carnivorous depending on political allegiance.

"Charismatic. Erratic. Beloved. Feared. Transformative visionary. Radical reductionist. Bold leader. Alienating isolationist. Bo Statler has been called all of these things. Whatever your view, it is clear he has pushed this country further than any of his predecessors. The results have been interpreted in wildly different ways, as has become the way of all things in this fractured Republic.

"His former colleagues in the Democratic party demonize him as a traitor and a deranged, reckless conman.

"His current Republican colleagues profess a strong working relationship but are never seen with him.

"Conservatives doubt his motives. Liberals warn he will bring about Armageddon.

"The media confirms a dozen versions of these positions depending on their specialty audiences.

"And we each must wade through this morass of spin and politicking and gibberish searching for the truth, which has long been on the endangered-species list.

"The questions we must ask ourselves in the face of all that has happened these past few decades is, 'Are we the Americans we dreamed we would be?' And I would add, do we understand what it really means if our answer is 'yes' – especially as our former allies burn?"

She stared silently out of his television for a moment, as if waiting for Bob to answer, and then said, "We'll be right back."

Steve lay down in a way that looked like he had fainted.

"Amy girl, sometimes you are just too intense for Steve," Bob spoke to the screen, raising one of his battered remotes. He clicked away from Amy to William Truth, another DVR mainstay. Old Will had an equally pronounced viewpoint, and a primetime show on National News. The lined face smirked ruefully over a blue pinstriped suit, sharp eyes glaring a challenge.

"Any fool who dares doubt the dignity and diligence of our President is not a True American, and should be treated accordingly," he said, managing to sound insistent, demanding, and dismissive at the same time. Bob knew his fans loved that about him.

"We re-elected our President as an expression of where we want our country to go and we should celebrate his patriotic repurposing of our resources and rewriting of our national mission statement."

"After hacking election rolls, of course," Bob murmured.

"Anyone who does not support our President... well, the door's right past Lady Liberty," Will sneered. And then he leaned forward just as Amy had. "Start swimming."

As if in response, Steve leapt off the couch and strutted into the kitchen.

"Don't be so close minded, ya snob," Bob called after him. "We need to be open to all sides of the conversation or where will we be?"

The only response was the sound of Steve lapping water from his dish.

"Drinking's never the answer, Steve."

Bob clicked around the vast wasteland of cable stations approved to broadcast anything but news or political discussion. He did this for a while without registering anything that flashed before his eyes, until he landed on a familiar sight: the marble statue of Lincoln thundering down the steps of his own memorial, using one of its columns to swat at tourists.

A much younger Bob stumbled onscreen, one of the stars of *Monster Cops*.

Younger Bob looked up in awe and murmured, "Well, *that* wasn't in the brochure."

Lincoln was followed by a swarm of power-suited werewolves. Shambling after them was a pack of zombies with cameras and microphones.

"And I thought it was too on the nose back then," Older Bob said.

Younger Bob shot an alarmed look at Lionel Jackson, his costar. "Who the hell are the suits?"

Jackson gave his signature scowl. "Can't you recognize Congress?"

"Explains the press."

Older Bob picked up the freshly hydrated dog, placed him on the couch, "Who knew we were making a documentary, Steve?"

Steve rolled over, facing away from the TV.

"Point made," Bob sighed, condemning Young Bob to cable oblivion as he clicked on into the night.

Chapter 5

WINSTON MILLER, HOST AND executive producer of *Miller Time*, the up-and-coming late night talk show threatening to overtake both *The Tonight Show* and *The Late Show's* ratings, was not pleased. His trademark grin was replaced with a carnivorous scowl.

Standing in front of his famed writers' table, Miller snarled at the mounted screen, "What do you mean you can't get your client for us, Jeremy?" He turned to his writers, "What do you think happened to Jeremy, guys?"

Onscreen, Jeremy visibly gulped.

"I think an old guy just took his manhood."

"Castrated him."

"His office door should read Emasculated Jeremy."

Miller held up a hand and the comments stopped. He stepped forward so his entire face filled Jeremy's monitor. "Get Bob Murphy on my show or I'll spend a year burying you in every night's monologue. You'll be famous in the very worst way possible. Understand me, Eunich?"

As Jeremy began answering, Miller cut the feed, turned to his staff. "We need Bob Murphy," he said. After a moment's thought, he snapped his fingers. "Get Sanderson! I want full hackage!"

The writers looked worried. "Boss, we only hack on

celebrity criminals...."

"He's being criminally negligent to his fans," Miller smiled darkly. "We're gonna find us a way to reel in this Great White Whale." He spread his arms wide. "Call me Ishmael for this beloved Comedy Icon right here! Boys, we are going fishing!"

Chapter 6

BOB WAS STANDING IN the kitchen eating Cheerios when his phone jumped to life, bebopping a bouncy tune. He placed the bowl in the sink, chewed and swallowed quickly, wiping milk off his mouth with the back of his hand as he opened up FaceTime.

"POP-POP!" His grandkids screamed from their end of the connection.

"Suzie-Kalloozie and RobbaDobba!"

The kids laughed. Bob joined them.

"I'm so glad you two called! What's going on? Tell me everything!"

Both of them launched into updates simultaneously, neither stopping nor caring that the other was talking. Bob nodded his head, entirely focused on following both of them. When they finished, he gushed, "Great achievements, both of you. Spelling Bees are tough and so are intramural sports. Suzie-Kalloozie Rules! RobbaDoobba is King! You two are my heroes!"

They shrieked in delight, drowning out the voice behind them. It repeated itself. "Okay, okay, can I speak to my dad, please?"

The kids protested, then blew kisses, their little faces still full of laughter, and then the view blurred with motion before coming to rest on his son's face.

God, he looks so much like Mary Angeline.

"Hey, Pop," Jackson said.

"Hey," Bob smiled. "Suzie and Rob are getting so big."

"You saw them just two weekends ago, Pop."

"Which is why I must suspect steroids," Bob shot back, smirking. "Son, parenting is not a competition."

Jackson laughed. "I'll remind Veronica," he said. "How you doing? Eating all right? You aren't standing in the kitchen scarfing down bowls of Cheerios every night are you?"

Bob wiped his mouth and chin as casually as possible, trying his best to be subtle. "It was steak tonight," he said. "Grilled it up with sautéed onions, a baked potato, and some steamed asparagus."

"You hate asparagus."

"That was for Steve."

"You can't live on cereal and pizza, Pop."

Bob deflected, "Who eats that combination? Dear God, what are you feeding my grandchildren?"

Robbie, off camera, screamed, "Poop!"

Jackson looked down and to his left in full dad mode. "Robert!"

Offscreen, Robbie mumbled. "Sorry, Dad."

"Don't apologize, RobbaDobba. Your dad should not be serving you poop!"

The kids giggled wildly, stopping short when their dad scowled. Finally, Jackson cracked a smile for them. Everybody laughed.

"Life is good," he said into the phone, "even if my son feeds my grandkids poop." Beautiful kids' laughter exploded again. A cheap milking of the punchline, he knew, but anything for his grandkids.

Chapter 7

PRESIDENT STATLER STEWED IN the White House movie theater where he watched the illegal news shows and kicked custom-made chairs every time a statement pissed him off. Two incurred expensive damage during tonight's viewing of *The Amy Brooks Update*.

"How does she get to go on every night and spout such pure hate?" Bo boomed. "Didn't we declare her kind enemies of the state?"

"We did, sir," said his Chief of Staff, Simon Wentworth. "She and her cohorts broadcast from secure locations."

Onscreen, Amy leaned forward. "Charismatic. Erratic. Beloved. Feared. Transformative visionary. Radical reductionist. Bold leader. Alienating isolationist. President Beauregard 'Bo' Statler has been called all of these for decades...."

Wentworth, who watched with him every evening to keep Bo from making angered proclamations on social media, reached for the President's gleaming remote. "Perhaps a comedy would be more enjoyable, Mr. President," he offered. "They are running Bob Murphy movies on HBO all this month. You always enjoy his films."

Statler swatted his hand away, never taking his eyes off the screen. Slouched in his seat, POTUS seethed,

"Can't we arrest her for treason?"

"Only if we can find her, sir."

"Find her then! Find her, shoot her, make it look like suicide, with a note apologizing for being so wrong about me," Bo demanded. "Hey! I should tweet that."

"Better I just forward your orders to the TASE, sir."

"Good job, Wentworth," Bo said, sated for the moment. He stared at Amy onscreen, growing calmer. "Find her," he murmured. "End her." Bo smiled. "Then I'll eulogize her misguided but admirable American spirit to demonstrate the benevolence of True Americans."

Chapter 8

THE MEADOWS.

Again.

Soft breeze. Blue skies. Sunshine. Tall grass. Her favorite blue picnic blanket. Those crackers from Pop's that she likes so much, with Monterey Jack cheese cut small enough to sit neatly on top. Some chilled prosecco, her favorite, in champagne flutes. Mary Angeline looking up with those intoxicating brown eyes — the only eyes ever to look at him that way — a little embarrassed because she knows he's staring.

How breathtaking she is, even at their age.

Once again, he needs to kiss that impossibly tiny mouth, to once more experience all that is right in his world.

They move toward each other —

Bob awoke in their bed, the moon's placid glow turning their boudoir a soft, empty blue.

He sighed. Like he did every night. Because he dreamed of her every night.

He sat up and saw Steve. Usually, the dog slept on Mary Angeline's pillow until the wee hours when Bob woke up and the ritual began. Tonight, he was already there, curled up in a little bed Bob had placed on his late wife's dresser right under the nearly life size wedding portrait, directly below Mary Angeline.

It was as close as Steve could get to her now.

Bob stared at it as had become his ritual, the portrait somehow offering both dog and man comfort in this desolate time of night.

It was as close as Bob could get to her now.

At first he had resisted the portrait. He thought that hanging a huge picture of them in their home seemed vain. When she sensed his resistance, she grew quiet, never one to argue. But when Mary Angeline became quiet Bob's world trembled. So huge portrait it was.

He ignored it for years, walking by the pretentious thing day after day. If he saw her admiring the photograph, he was happy to gush over how gorgeous she was in it, but for Bob, Mary Angeline defined beauty wherever she was, so why did he need an imitation of that splendor hanging over the living room couch?

To Bob, the portrait was hers.

And then, it wasn't.

Nothing was.

He had opened his entire world to her and Mary Angeline had immeasurably improved all of it, until the vicious Fates decided such blessings no longer amused them.

But before they cursed him, it had all been glory.

As Bob's career reached dizzying heights, he experienced guilt over their obscene wealth. Mary Angeline suggested a charity to fund relief efforts to countries hit by natural disasters.

And so Gratitude Unlimited was born. They launched it using 40 percent of their wealth. His accountant was apoplectic.

When Bob was home, they'd organize huge televised comedy specials to raise even more funds for the charity. When he was away, Mary Angeline would travel to heartbreaking locations and without fanfare pitch in to help the efforts she was financing. Sometimes it was delivering medicine to fight an outbreak of some disease. Increasingly, it was recovery efforts after the latest hurricane, earthquake, or tsunami. Always reported as "once in a century" these devastating events hit every few months. National News might refuse to report it as the result of escalating climate change, but the dead and the newly homeless knew better.

And then president Bo decided no one should help foreign countries "until they pay their fair share," whatever the hell that meant. In her quietly independent way, Mary Angeline continued to fund and participate in relief efforts anyway, speaking about "putting people over politics" whenever National News demanded an explanation.

Stupidly, Bob was proud instead of worried.

He had underestimated the president, a mistake that would be his undoing.

It was what Gratitude Unlimited staff called "a deliver and run trip" to a disease-ravaged part of the Third World. Mary Angeline and her team were forbidden to go, but their plane was private, the flight plan could be faked, so what would be the harm in saving thousands against some politician's wishes? Further, medical experts assured them they could be on the ground for up to four hours before the plane's self-contained atmosphere would get infected, and the plan was for them to be in country no more than 90 minutes. It would be easier to apologize than ask permission.

Or so they thought.

The president weaponized that private plane against Gratitude Unlimited, and with a small bribe to the government of that country, stranded them for five days.

Five days.

The entire relief team was declared a national health risk and barred from re-entering The States.

"They were warned," National News reported, "but Hollywood egos won't listen to the wisdom of our leaders."

The Red Cross, now a Canadian organization after it was banned for violating similar national policies, eventually airlifted the Gratitude Unlimited team out of that hellhole. Bob flew to France where they were taken for treatment.

It was too late. Bo's plan had worked perfectly. Another of his perceived enemies had been dealt with.

Bob sat by Mary Angeline's side imprisoned in a contamination suit, unable to touch his beloved as she used all of her fading energy to call medical experts around the globe trying to save her team. By the time the last of them died, Bob had been forced to witness every aspect of his stunning wife wither to barely more than a skeleton.

And then it was only Bob and Mary Angeline, her bedridden, him in that damned suit.

The fragrance of the flowers piled high outside the hospital window couldn't reach them. Headlines couldn't reach them. Presidential orders for Bob to return couldn't reach them. French officials misdirected True American ambassadors away from Murphy's location, sending them to all parts of the country.

The medical staff granted them privacy, which they used to stare into each other's shattered eyes, beyond prayer, beyond hope, suspended in the long, slow dusk of their time together.

He was reciting her favorite Shakespearean sonnet when the end came.

"... thy eternal summer shall not fade. Nor lose possession of that fair ...."

Mary Angeline's frail grip on his gloved hand loosened.

And she was gone.

Chapter 9

THAT MOMENT ECHOED OUT across his suddenly meaningless life.

The unfairness, the cruelty, the brutal, unrelenting reality darkened every minute of every hour of his now worthless existence.

And she had left him the mutt, too. That Sasha. Ridiculous little creature. He remembered asking himself, after the funeral, once he returned to his now hollow home, how was he going to take care of a dog when he couldn't even bring himself to eat?

He realized he wouldn't. They could both fade out together. Fine by him. Mary Angeline might be glad to see them again so soon....

He was resolved to die, haunting the house in an aimless shamble, growing weaker, wandering closer to what he wanted more than anything.

Days into this slow suicide shuffle, he passed out on the couch and she came to him ... brought him to their first picnic....

He was sure he had died and this was heaven, or, acknowledging his own dodgy past, a fairly enjoyable purgatory.

Then he awoke just shy of that kiss, and cried for hours.

Night after night, there she was, his Mary Angeline,

just for a moment, and each night he moved toward just one ... more ... delicate ... kiss....

Bob allowed himself a drink of water, and eventually coffee, just to get him through the hours until the next dream. He tossed the mutt a few scraps but still couldn't force himself to eat.

He was not sure how many days passed. Then one night he fell off the couch reaching for her. Slammed his chin on the coffee table, saw stars, drew blood, and then just laid there pathetically staining the carpet, crippled by the loss of her again.

Looking around the room cursing himself for being too weak to end this wretched sham and rejoin her, he saw the mutt, that Sasha.

The mutt was not looking at Bob.

Instead he was curled up on the top of the couch, right under that huge portrait.

More correctly, the dog was directly under the right side of that immense wedding photos, beneath his Mary Angeline in shimmering white, love radiating from the most soulful, beautiful, life-affirming eyes he had ever seen.

Bob rose and eased closer, taking in the portrait as if for the first time.

The dog glanced at Bob, and then settled back in as he had on her lap hundreds of times throughout their years together.

Bob glanced at Sasha (what a horrible name) and then returned his gaze to his wife. He stared at her image for a long while, and, for the first time in what seemed an eternity, he felt a little better.

Eventually, the dog yawned and turned its surprisingly appealing face to him.

"Wanna eat?" Bob asked.

"Yip," the dog replied.

"Gotta eat," Bob said, taking the cute little creature into his arms. As they approached the kitchen together, Bob gave the dog serious consideration. He was a handsome little dude, but definitely a guy. "We gotta do something about that name, bro," Bob told him, placing the dog on a chair. "How about Steve?"

"Yip."

"Steve it is."

They had their first real meal then and it became their new nightly ritual: the dream, the pain, the portrait, and then a shared meal. Eventually, Bob moved the portrait into their bedroom and got a doggy bed. He placed it under her side of that beautiful picture.

And every night at some point the dog would look at him with those soulful brown eyes and he'd know why Mary Angeline had left the Yorkie with him.

"Yeah, bro," Bob would say, "I miss her too."

Chapter 10

SOMETIMES AFTER THE DREAM, when neither could get back to sleep, Steve and Bob sat on the couch and watched TV. Tonight was another DVR marathon. Lots of Amy Brooks. In this episode she was in front of a curtain rather than her flimsy studio set. Bob interpreted the changes as times Amy had been forced to relocate quickly, abandoning her desk and backdrop. Eventually another would be slapped together, but soon that would be abandoned too.

"Amy is flirting with disaster, Steve," he said.

Steve took the fifth.

Onscreen, Amy showed a clip from an infomercial Bob had skipped over on many a night. But if Amy wanted to talk about it, that was fine with him and Steve.

"Medafree liberates you from the constraints people suffered under Medicare and Medicaid!" The unseen commercial narrator seemed thrilled to be sharing this revelation with over Amy's shoulder. "With Medafree you can be confident that should there be a severe medical problem, all your very expensive medical care will be covered."

Cut to Amy with a still from the commercial over her right shoulder. She was as intense as ever, leaning forward, her gleaming black hair interrupted only by that shock of white, both enhancing the brilliance of her penetrating blue eyes. "There's something else to know about this coverage, this promised worry-free coverage, this alleged improvement on Medicaid and Medicare. Evidence coming to light today makes a strong case that Medafree actually liberates many patients from getting any treatment at all. Additionally, it is being reported that any treatment the lucky few do get comes at a higher co-pay than any ever incurred with Medicaid or Medicare.

"That is correct; little or no actual treatment received after inhumane waits and at higher costs than ever before.

"Besides all that, the Harvard Medical Center has just released a study suggesting —with a daunting amount of irrefutably well-documented evidence — that there has been a shocking spike in 'inoperable' cancer cases and 'inoperable' liver problems and 'inoperable' heart disease since Medafree was enacted.

"This spike in 'inoperable' diagnoses comes at a time when science has been making incredible breakthroughs in medicine for three decades. And the numbers are staggering. Almost historical. You want to know when, in the entire history of humanity, there have been more inoperable conditions?

"During the Black Plague.

"It is almost as if medical professionals are being forced to pump patients full of mass produced pain killers and put them in a very clean, very nice, far more cost-efficient hospice environment where they can die peacefully stoned rather than incur the massive costs of true healthcare.

"The allegations we're hearing is that while

Medafree patients think they're free from excessive costs, those who know say they also seem to be free of medical help."

Amy smirked into the camera. "But, as so many thousands of tweets and Facebook posts allege every day, this is probably all left-leaning, pathetically hysterical socialist fear mongering.

"You might be right. But just in case...."

Amy paused, her brilliant blue eyes reaching out to the world with an amazing mixture of intensity and challenge, and then she whispered a bit theatrically, "...don't get sick."

Bob sunk into his couch a little deeper and whispered, "Too late."

Chapter 11

LATER, STEVE AND BOB found themselves watching another episode of Amy, in front of a different makeshift set (the Feds must be in hot pursuit) as she introduced a clip from *All Sides Included*, the only show with a non-white host on National News. The clip showed a man who at one time would have been described as Arab-American, interviewing a white guy who at one time would have been described as a redneck Aryan racist.

The white guy was saying, "What my brothers and I are talking about is that we can all live together. There is a place for each and every one of us. But it comes down to blood and soil; the simple truth is that all the top spots are reserved for whites, as it should be. Your hosting position here may amuse your betters, but you will not replace us. We are united, one nation, with no use for immigration. This land is our land, and it always has been."

Instead of replying, the talk show host looked to his right as a spokesman for the United Native Americans Council (also now housed in Canada) walked onset in full tribal regalia, saying, "I beg to differ."

The white guy leapt to his feet. "This interview is over! I'm not going to be assaulted by your underhanded, aggressively racist strategies, nor am I going to entertain the claims from this invader to our shores! God Bless America!"

He stormed off set.

The scene cut to Amy in yet another studio. "That was National News' *All Sides Included* with host Abdun Ahmed, the only person of color on staff throughout that entire network. That clip was from two days ago. Tonight, Abdun Ahmed was assaulted while on a daily jog through his Upper West Side neighborhood."

She glanced at her notes, continued. "According to many eyewitnesses, a group of white males leapt from a rented van, beat him with crowbars and then jumped back into the van and drove off. Ahmed is in critical condition at Mount Sinai Hospital."

Amy did her signature intense look into the camera. "It's all there in the Bill of Rights. At the number one spot. Freedom of religion, speech, and the press. Right there at number one."

Amy Brooks paused, taking in a deep breath, eyes cast down as if in thought, that white streak in her hair gleaming in the studio lights. "God bless America," she said and then raised her gaze to the camera with all the sympathy she could push out of those electric blue, tear-filled eyes. Something broke in her voice as she murmured, "Please."

Chapter 12

BOB WOKE UP ON the couch, the morning news blaring. The Weather Guy was wrapping up. "That's our five-day forecast. And remember everyone, it's National Secretary Day, so be kind to those who service you so well. Here's to you, Sue."

As the screen cut to a startled Sue, Bob gave the screen a double take and then stumbled toward the kitchen. "Steve, did you make coffee? It is your turn, bro."

Onscreen, Sue recovered, and with an overcompensating smile launched into the next story. "An as yet unidentified man was being beaten by four other men outside a Muscle Bros Workout Emporium in Brooklyn yesterday, when, to their surprise, two large gym patrons ran out and subdued the attackers, sending all four assailants to the emergency room after they 'resisted citizen's arrest', according to witnesses."

Sue shifted to another camera angle. "Police took statements from over a dozen of those witnesses, and then declined to charge the sweat-suited Samaritans. But only hours later, lawyers posted bail for all four alleged assailants and filed lawsuits against the NYPD, the city, the mayor, the witnesses, the gym guys, Muscle Bros Workout Emporium, and the unidentified man who remains in critical condition."

In the kitchen, Bob found an empty milk carton in the fridge. "Damn it," he murmured, and then called out loudly, "Steve, we gotta go to Pop's. Are you putting the recycling in the baskets or are you gonna stick me with the manual labor again?" After a pause he called out once more, "I figured as much, you prima donna!"

Chapter 13

AT POP'S THEY BOUGHT milk, eggs, maple syrup, and that 12-grain bread Mary Angeline had turned him on to years ago.

Pop rang up the items making small talk, though today his efforts sounded a bit forced. "Making French toast today? Must be Steve's turn to cook."

"That's what the calendar says, but somebody's been dodging the issue all morning," Bob shot a glance at his buddy happily chomping a treat.

Usually, Pop would "admonish" Steve, joking that the tiny dog needed to pull his weight. But today he just focused on bagging the items.

Bob glanced at the calendar and suddenly understood. He busied himself checking the contents of one of the bags and whispered, "How long?"

"Five, today," Pop whispered back, packing another bag, failing at a smile.

Five years....

"True Americanism" grew over the decade, with Congress eventually expanding from the debrowning of America to additionally target certain lifestyles that suddenly posed a threat to the True American Way of Life. Lightning quick changes in law began working to strip away LBGTQIA rights to assemble in public and rent legitimate housing. Eventually, a law was enacted to crack down on "public disruptions" (broadly interpreted to include everything from dressing in drag to looking attracted to members of the same sex in public).

Buried deep in the bill sat a paragraph that outlawed all non-procreational sexual preferences, which, once all the legal babble about keeping America focused on our unified True American goals was peeled away, made the very existence of all LGBTQIA people illegal.

The new laws identified as targets, according to Bo, "any undesirables in possession of obviously faked American birth certificates and other false papers because True Americans, by definition, cannot be criminals or rapists or murderers or thieves or socialists or terrorists or gays or trans or queers or unsure about their sexuality. True Americans know who they are and what their God-given destiny is, and, by the love of our all-powerful Father in Heaven, we are going to protect True Americans from this filth."

Pop's son Terence was gay, and smart enough to see the storm clouds gathering. He took off months before True Americans Day.

At first, Pop regularly received cards from Terry postmarked Canada or Europe, other times he would get a call, but since True Americans Day, there had only been silence. Terence knew it would put his parents in danger to contact them.

Bob whispered, "You know that if there is anything I can do—"

Pop cut him off with a raised eyebrow and a quick glance at the television. "Gonna watch the big game?"

The place was bugged, or Pop suspected as much, which amounted to the same thing. These days, no one was willing to take a chance.

Bob nodded.

The coldest aspect of True Americans Day was the launching of a reality show that premiered that very night on National News. *Patriotism Live* featured regular, everyday people hunting down "defilers of the American Dream" for bounties.

Humans hunting humans. For cash prizes. On government-sponsored national television.

No rules were set for how "prey" were to be hunted or captured, and the show was broadcast later in the evening to accommodate potential (pronounced "guaranteed") graphic violence.

Contestants were known to show up at the homes or businesses of the families of their prey. And it was widely suspected that the government supplied these leads, supposedly from tech observation. The widespread belief was that bugs had been installed in all later model technology, appliances, and vehicles. Any snippet of private dialogue could wind up on the show, and the public did not seem to be alarmed. After all, it never happened to True Americans.

Often violent interrogations would be filmed with the resulting "volunteered information" leading to the prey being "apprehended" live on television.

Patriotism Live enjoyed even higher ratings than major sports events. If reported ratings were to be believed, most True Americans watched every episode.

And, much to their shame, so did Pop and Bob.

Each week, they searched for any sign of Terence just as families across these wrecked states watched for signs of their own fugitive loved ones. Each prayed they would find no trace, but still couldn't stay away, just in case. And they all hated themselves for not being strong enough to turn the channel.

And now Bob may have given them away.

"I'm sure he's ... we're ... okay," Bob whispered.

"I'm sure none of us are," Pop murmured back.

They stood in awkward silence. There was nothing else to say, and a real danger in saying anything at all. Finally, Bob took his bags, ashamed that his mind screamed at him to get out, get away, get home where he would be safe. To hide this, he nodded to the storeowner and mouthed, "Stay strong."

Pop nodded, and then leaned over the counter to wag a finger at the dog. "It's your turn to cook, Steve. Pull your weight, boy."

Bob held the door open for the little dog, his cheeks burning at his fear, forcing himself to cast one more look at Pop, knowing all his movie star money couldn't buy back Terrence's safety; there was not a single thing he could do or say without risking himself.

Coward.

Chapter 14

AS BOB LEFT THE store, his shame shifted to anger. "Not you again."

Jeremy stood outside Pop's bearing gifts.

Behind him stood a dog groomer, a dog grooming truck, a folding table laden with *Monster Cop* Blu Rays, and a sign that read, "I know I wasn't invited to be here but may I PLEASE have a minute?"

"Jeremy, you have the worst timing in the world," Bob said through clinched teeth.

"Please, Mr. Murphy. Please, please, please can I speak to you?" Jeremy even clasped his hands in prayer and held them up to his chest. "Giovanni here can pamper Steve while we talk."

Bob forgot how young Jeremy actually was, but he looked about 18 now. Realistically, he had to be in his late twenties, still young for such a savage business. This was probably his first professional job and they took one look at his inability to drink the blood of his competitors and assigned him to the aging recluse.

Bob remembered how raw he had been at that age, how his career would have ended right on the Second City stage except for the kindness of one audience member. And here was this kid clearly sweating through what might easily be the final moments of his dream career.

Bob looked down at Steve, "Wanna get a mani-padi?"

Steve seemed skeptical until Giovanni opened a jar of Milk-Bone Mini Beef, Chicken, and Bacon Flavored Snacks. The jar was bigger than the dog. Steve took one whiff and went right over.

"He could be a dognapper and you don't care," Bob chuckled. "You're a shameless Milk-Bone ho."

He turned to the folding table of Blu-Rays. "And I'm supposed to be equally thrilled about these?"

Jeremy raised his hands, palms out. "Here's my idea; if you want, we'll give them out free to your neighbors — ask them to decide whether all the extras make repurchasing the movie worthwhile. If they say yes, you do the appearances."

"No," Bob said.

"Please, Bob," Jeremy pleaded. "Winston Miller's really pissed. I could lose my job."

"Pop can give them out, use them for coasters, whatever, but we are not using my neighbors as beta testers."

"Does this mean you'll do the appearances?"

Bob put his groceries into the shopping baskets attached to the back of his bike. "The deal was all of this for a minute. Time's up."

Jeremy's eyes actually filled with tears, his breath jerked shakily in and out of his chest, his lip quivered. He noticed Steve with his tiny head tilted up, eyes closed, leaning into an apparently epic brush massage. "S-Steve's not f-finished yet! C-can we keep talking?"

Bob folded his arms, pissed that Jeremy was making him feel bad for not wanting to do the whore tour. "Go," he said.

"Okay, goodgoodgood," the young executive was scrambling, and Bob let him flounder. "All we need to do is figure out what would make you comfortable."

"Staying at home makes me comfortable."

"Great! We can have them interview you in your home!"

"Not unless they want to get shot."

"But, but ... you've always said you're a pacifist."

"My neighbor Merle is not."

"Um." After a moment, a bit of the old hotshot surfaced. "We'll have to bring the sheriff, then."

"That would be Merle. Not a huge fan of mine, but he holds to the law."

Jeremy's façade collapsed, eyes welling anew. "What would you prefer then?

"I prefer to be left alone."

Jeremy's voice cracked, desperate words tumbling out. "And I'd love to do that for you, Mr. Murphy, I really would, but I have college debt coming out my ass, loans my parents cosigned because they love me and I was too naïve to understand that the sonofabitch banker was mortgaging my family's future, betting we wouldn't be able to pay it off. And my parents are not going to lose the house they slaved to own because of me! I'm sorry, but they are not. And all I'm asking, Bob — Mr. Murphy — Sir — all I'm really asking is for you to allow yourself to get chauffeured to some TV studios, allow your fans to adore you just one more time, and share some memories of one of the highlights of your professional career."

"I know that's what you think you are asking for—"

Jeremy cut him off. "Am I really that far off base? Are you worried about being rusty? You're funny with me all the time."

"Different kind of funny."

"This is my life on the line here! I don't get this done, I get fired. I get fired, I can't pay my loans. I can't pay my loan, my parents lose their home—"

Bob shrugged again. "I'll pay off your loans."

An impressive fury exploded from the young man. "I DON'T WANT YOU TO PAY MY BILLS! I DON'T WANT MY PARENTS TO PAY MY BILLS! I WANT —FOR ONCE IN MY GODDAMN LIFE — TO ACCOMPLISH SOMETHING ON MY OWN!"

The words echoed out across the quiet streets. A few lights went on in windows. Bob and Jeremy and Giovanni and Steve froze in the awkward aftermath.

Pop came out of the store. "Everything all right out here?"

Bob spoke quietly, taking one of the Blu Rays. "These are yours to give out to whomever still has a player. No catch. Or you can use them for skeet practice."

Pop tapped the movies. "Been meaning to get in some shooting."

Bob tipped Giovanni. Then secured the newly fab Steve into his basket at the front of the bike. "You ready, Handsome?"

Steve preened a bit.

Bob straddled the mutated two-wheeler. He glanced at Jeremy. "I'll think about it," he said, and then pushed off, pedaling down the street toward home silhouetted in the rising sun.

Chapter 15

SANDERSON DIDN'T TAKE LONG to get back to Miller with a report. "Ain' much," he said, hunching his shoulders in a "whuddoya want from me" attitude. A hacker specializing in obtaining personal information, he projected his findings across a wall in Miller's office. "Bob Murphy's activity over the last few years," Sanderson said.

Bike routes. Interior shots of Bob's home. Video of Steve running around the back yard. Ignored email accounts. Activity sheets for Twitter, Facebook, other social-media sites, all but one unused by Bob himself. Shopping lists and bills from Pop's.

"He's practically off the grid," Sanderson shrugged. "Has a presence online that is maintained by some law office in LA, but he has never interacted with any of it himself. Tortures that rookie his film company sends out to him on the regular, never agrees to anything. Hasn't posted anywhere since his wife kicked. This guy is DOA."

Miller shot him a look.

Sanderson smirked, proud of his acronym. "Dead Online Always."

Miller studied the wall, pouring over documents and details. "Always?"

Sanderson smirked. "Except for FaceTiming with

his grandkids."

Miller grinned, punched a number into his phone. "Send up Gus from Tech. No, it's gotta be Gus." His smile widened. "Sanderson, you're a gift from God."

Sanderson ginned like a raptor. "'Ain' much' is usually enough."

Chapter 16

STEVE AND BOB ARRIVED home in time to prepare for a visit from the local handyteen and his precious sidekick — a highpoint of their social schedule.

A few years back, Sheriff Merle's son, answering to Merle Junior at the time, had come around looking for work. Bob "hired" the boy to pull weeds in the spring and rake leaves in the fall. The rates increased as the years passed (it started at a dollar and a plate of cookies), as did the challenges of dealing with the boy as he mutated from a cute kid into ... many other things.

The consistently best part of this particular business arrangement was his sidekick — an adorable little girl. When they first started coming over, Mary Angeline instantly fell in love with the then three-year-old Perri.

Bob suspected it was a cheap childcare scheme on the part of that wily Sheriff Merle, but Mary Angeline loved having them over, so Bob let it slide. Later he discovered Merle's wife had left them, which made Mary Angeline Perri's only female role model, another reason to embrace their time at the Murphy house.

Mary Angeline and the baby bonded over a mutual love of flowers, inspiring his wife to start a garden, which they worked on together during each visit. Perri's pigtails bounced as she watered everything with a sprinkler can Mary Angeline bought for her. Everything. More than once the little darling had watered Bob's work boots if he was careless enough to leave them on the porch steps.

After Mary Angeline passed, the pair kept coming around, the boy using the excuse that Perri wanted to keep the garden going in Mary Angeline's memory. As the girl wasn't more than five at the time, Bob suspected there were other reasons but he was too shattered to challenge anyone on anything. Perri ordered supplies from him by announcing, "We'll need new seeds soon, and fresh dirt (she meant soil). That's how Aunt Mary always did it."

Every time she invoked Mary Angeline as aunt, Perri got anything she wanted. Bob took to writing down shopping lists from the itsy bitsy boss, especially when she spoke to him with her hands on her hips, head tilted slightly to the right — Mary Angeline's "all business" posture.

The embers of Bob's life glowed a bit brighter every time Perri looked at the results, nodding her little angel face in approval exactly as Mary Angeline used to.

The son's presence on Bob's property, however, seemed to piss off the sheriff. One day, he suggested Bob was trying to lure his boy into the house for nefarious purposes. After a furious exchange, Bob said the kids never went into the house, preferring the porch and the garden, but if the sheriff wanted to upset Perri he could keep them away.

That knocked the authoritarian accusation out of the law officer's voice. "Look, I know it's bad with your wife gone," he muttered. "Been hell for us since Wilma took off with ... on her own adventures. Merle Junior has been suffering the most. Blames himself for her leaving. Confused him all to hell."

The two men looked at Sheriff Merle's children in the garden; Perri, eight-years-old then, kneeling and digging delicately in her "gardening outfit" – Mary Angeline's red rubber boots (too big for Perri, but Bob could never tell her no about anything), a blue jumper with the white polka dots, Mary Angeline's old gardening gloves (which went up over Perri's elbows), and the bandana Mary Angeline had given her, tied around her soft curls just as Bob's beloved had taught her.

Steve sat by her whenever Perri did her gardening.

Now 16, Merle Junior still stood guard over his sister, handing the little one seeds upon command. But the changes he'd undergone had been numerous and dramatic.

"Merle Junior ain't been Merle Junior for going on three years," the sheriff said. "He was Mu'Laluth for while during his H.P. Lovecraft phase, and then Merna during an ... ah ... experimental phase. Now he insists on being called ... well you know."

"I've been here for all of the changes," Bob acknowledged quietly.

"Phases," the sheriff insisted, looking a hundred years old, exhaling slowly before speaking. "I was FBI before this job. I've taken down drug cartels, and terrorists, and serial killers ... but ... I can't understand my own son."

The sheriff glanced at Bob and then moved his eyes quickly away. "Maybe an outside influence might get him to ... find some balance."

Sheriff Merle nodded to himself, exhaled, nodded

to Bob, and then hurried off, the situation somehow resolved.

So the kids were allowed to work Perri's garden on Bob's property, which was going to happen today. And that meant one thing.

Thanos, scourge of the galaxy, was coming.

To clean out Bob's gutters.

And maybe find an Infinity Stone.

Chapter 17

BOB PUT THE GROCERIES away, tossed the purloined copy of *Monster Cop* on the couch, and set to whipping up French toast.

He turned on the small TV in the kitchen. *The All-American News with Bling Holston* was on National News. She was coiffed beyond any logic and spoke with detached importance. "Yet another weakling teacher has taken his own life, Los Angeles police report."

Bob took out specially ordered wheat and rye bread he had waited a month for, eggs, butter, and cinnamon.

Onscreen, Bling turned to another camera angle, comporting herself with even more importance from this vantage point. "Pathetically, Adam Nelson was found hanging, with a suicide note scribbled sloppily on an otherwise promising American Way catalog. The catalog is sent to schools across the nation. In it, companies generously help American Way High School English teachers, actually providing lesson plans for this privileged part-time profession.

"According to his principal, Nelson's copy was opened to a model lesson plan offering this great essay question: 'What would Romeo and Juliet order from this catalog to be among the best dressed in their kingdoms during their torrid romance?'

Bling shook her lush locks, luxuriously disappointed.

"Prospering business leaders were doing his job for him, and this guy had problems? Give me a break.

"This Nelson joins other classroom failures in death, including another English teacher from Plark Auto Parts High School in Utah; all that whiner had to do was have his students answer, 'What car would Claudius buy for Hamlet to help him get over his father's death?' Boom, done, and these losers complain.

"Good riddance, I say," Bling declared.

Bob had the stovetop going, heating his favorite pan as he mixed the eggs and added some milk.

Onscreen, the stunning blonde turned to yet another angle and another important expression. "President Bo Statler said that his stand on the situation continues."

The screen cut to Bo. "If we're honest with each other," he said, nodding compassionately, "this merely is a weeding out process for substandard educators. While it is heartbreaking and our condolences go out to the families now burdened with explaining this shameful act to the students, I'd have them remember that raising the next generation of True Americans is sacred work for which there is no higher calling. Not everybody is fit to teach our beloved children. I'd suggest to those students upset by the loss of this one to go see the football couch and get some pads. That surely helped me in my time as an All-County High School All-Star. It can help you too, kids."

Bob dipped rye bread into the batter. The egg-soaked bread hit the buttered pan with a sizzle. He flipped the bread slices as Mary Angeline had taught him. She was always so much better at it, he thought, better at everything. Bob slid the French toast onto plates, in a hurry now, calling out Mary Angeline's greeting for them as he placed the food on the porch table. "Ready or not here comes company!"

Indeed, Thanos, the Terror of Titan, slouched toward Bethlehem.

So did Perri.

Actually, she was skipping.

Chapter 18

IT WAS IMPOSSIBLE TO offer anything to Thanos because he was above all, but if he arrived when a hot plate of food was already on the porch table, he tended to claim it as tribute to his sovereignty.

Such was the fate of the first batch o'breakfast.

Thanos strode onto the porch wearing a faded purple shirt featuring a "self-portrait" across the entire front; a wide face with a malicious grin, an actual skull in the illustration's jet black eyes. Bob recognized the art style as belonging to Jim Starlin from way back in the trippy 70's. Cool. The human head that rose out of the top of that shirt, however, was distinctly unthreatening. Pale skin was pierced at the lip and the nose and multiple times along the left ear. His ginger hair had long since been dyed purple, because, you know, it struck fear in the hearts of the pathetic human race.

He sat with skinny legs set too far apart, toothpick arms circling the food with the swagger of much thicker and more terrifying limbs. He offered the smallest of chin nods before taking what was rightfully his, with lots of butter and syrup.

Perri tended to eat later, after her work was done. She preferred cotton candy-flavored ice cream with chunks of Reese's Peanut Butter cups and gummi bears, or had years ago when such treats had been available and Mary Angeline would feed them anything they wanted. These days it was toast with jelly.

Bob responded to Thanos' greeting with a solemn nod, delivering another plate of French toast to the table in case the one-time god of the universe was still hungry. He immediately returned to the kitchen and fed Steve to give the space warlord time to decide. When he got back to the porch two of the three additional slices of French toast were still on the plate. Thanos was digging into the other triumphantly.

With a cheek full of calories, the Terror of Titan benevolently indicated Bob was welcome to the remaining scrapes. "Join Thanos."

Bob sat, fought back a smirk. "You are too generous, my lord."

"Today we conquer your festering outer defenses," Thanos announced.

This was how Thanos approached chores, as enemies to conquer. Whatever cleared the gutters, bro. "Will the great Thanos be utilizing his flying throne or more earthbound elevation techniques?"

"The latter will suffice."

"Ladder it is," Bob confirmed.

They munched for a while and then Thanos got down to business. "What do you request of Thanos, the First? Know whom you address. You are in the presence of the Great Warrior!"

From her garden, Perri patted the soil lovingly and spoke almost in singsong. "Oohhhh great warrior! Wars not make one great. Teeheeheeheeheeheeheee!"

Bob did a double take. "Did she just quote Yoda?"

"I'm teaching her culture," the teen said, grinning, and momentarily dropping the façade. Then he turned to Perri, his defensive persona back in place. "Do you require my assistance, youngling?"

"Not yet."

The boy turned to Bob, "Voice your request, Earthman, before your better decides she requires the aid of Thanos."

"My lord, the request is that you climb up a ladder and clear out all the leaves and gunk clogging the gutters all around the house."

The boy shoved the last of Bob's French toast into his face, "Fihunnr."

"Nope, not worth five hundred."

"Die."

"Not today," Bob chuckled. "Twenty-five dollars or I do it myself."

"Fall and die, frail ancient mortal."

"I'm still pretty nimble for a geezer."

"Your life is forfeit to Thanos!"

"My life is forfeit to Thanos every time you come around here."

"As it should be."

"How come Steve's life is never forfeit to Thanos?"

"The dog has style."

Bob nodded his agreement, tossing Steve a treat. "So, are we going to get to work or is Thanos in a union?"

"Silence, whelp, or Thanos will lay waste to your soul!"

"Too late, kid."

The unexpected darkness from Bob threw the ruler of the galaxies off his game. The teenager emerged again, concerned. "You okay?"

"Good question," Bob answered, nodding slowly until a wiggle of his eyebrows got them laughing.

Chapter 19

THEY WORKED FOR HOURS, Bob steadying the
ladder whether the mighty Thanos needed it or not,
keeping an eye on Perri as they worked the gutters not
far from her garden. When they needed to go around
the house, Bob asked Perri if she would water the
bushes and flowerpots on each side (Mary Angeline had
placed flowers and plants all around the house, and she
and Perri would take care of all of them together back
when the world made sense). He checked on her often
to ensure the little cutie was always in his sight.

As they worked, the teenager sounded less like
Marvel comics' intergalactic tyrant and more like
Merle Junior. Small talk relaxed him. The topic never
mattered. What music was good these days. Which
shows were worth checking out. Whether there was any
actual meat in meatloaf any more. Which was funnier,
when the Mexicans bombed The Wall with catapults
full of feces or when Canadians built a wall of their own
to keep out fleeing Americans?

With each topic, the kid, tall and lanky at 16, became
more a kid and less of whatever he was tossing up as a
defense that day. While cleaning the gutter above Bob's
bedroom window, something caught Merle Junior's
eye. He stared through the glass for a long moment,
and then glanced at Bob, nodding his head toward the

window. "Was she righteous or a gold digger?"

Bob knew the kid had seen the portrait. "Mary Angeline was as righteous as they come."

"How could you tell?"

Relationship advice. That was new. Maybe Merle Junior had a crush. "First of all, I met her before anything happened for me," Bob spoke truthfully. "As a matter of fact, she saved me from failing out of comedy."

Merle climbed down the ladder, stripped off muck-covered gloves, and looked Bob right in the eye, something he never did. "How?"

"That's a tale best told over PB and J's."

Merle Jr. nodded. "Gotta eat."

"Gotta eat."

Chapter 20

BOB HAD BEEN SAVING his peanut butter stash, but since they were going to talk about Mary Angeline, it was a special occasion. He spread a modest amount across wheat bread with just a hint of jelly, and poured a big glass of milk. For Perri he made six Ritz crackers each with a dollop of peanut butter, into each of which he pressed a dent where he carefully placed a drop of jelly. Mary Angeline used to make them so much better, but Perri accepted his sloppier versions with admirable grace.

Merle Junior built a monstrosity. The bottom was a slice of seedless rye slathered with a thick spread of peanut butter. Next was a slice of pumpernickel bread covered in a diabetes-inducing blob of jelly, topped with a slice of wheat bread. He matched that mountain of calories with a pint glass of orange juice.

Bob laughed. "You are the Salvador Dali of sandwiches, my man."

"'If you are lucky enough to have lived in peanut butter as a young man, then wherever you go for the rest of your life it stays with you, for peanut butter is a movable feast,'" the kid said, raising the sandwich toward his mouth.

Bob raised his eyebrows. "Hemingway."

Merle Junior paused, pinkies holding up the corners

of the sandwich so the jelly couldn't escape. "Almost."

"You read a lot?"

"An assignment at Hamburger High," Merle Junior smirked. "Don't tell anyone."

Hamburger High was an apt nickname for his school. When Congress did away with public education funding in favor of for-profit charter schools, huge conglomerates and chain stores took them over as tax shelters and promotional vehicles. America's Way Department stores took west coast high schools. Plark Auto snapped up Utah and surrounding state high schools. And a certain fast food chain snapped up all the high schools in Illinois, Michigan, Pennsylvania, New Jersey and New York, thus the nickname.

Merle Junior took a huge bite of his absurd lunch, chewed awhile, swallowed, and washed it down with gulps of OJ. After wiping his face with a napkin, using exceptional manners, he nodded to Bob.

"Speaking of guarded secrets, check this out," Merle Junior said, thumbing his phone. He opened some app, showed Bob two video clips. The first was of citizens, and the second was President Statler, both showed people getting True American Security Implants.

"Yeah, saw this when it happened," Bob shrugged. "They say they'll get around to us by next spring."

"Watch again."

Merle Junior replayed both. The clip showed regular folk getting their True American Security Tracker Implants via an injection. As the shots were administered there was a "phmph" sound that made it seem even more painful. The other clip showed the president getting his in what had been a nationally televised moment. But in the Statler clip there was a beat and then the sound was heard.

"Hear that? Fake sound effect dropped in with poor timing," the kid announced.

Bob shrugged. "Back and to the left. Back and to the left."

"Laugh it up, fur ball, but this guy didn't get a tracker. He's full of shit."

Perri shot her brother a frown. "Language!"

"Sorry, Captain," he said, looking at Bob knowingly. "And?"

"Let's take this global. Expose him. End his horrible presidency."

"You can. I am not rebooting *All The President's Men.*"

"Who's gonna listen to me? Mr. Comedy Icon they'll listen to. America loves you."

"America loves that guy in the movies, the young one with the quips. That's not who I am any more."

Perri, focused on delicately picking up another peanut butter and jelly on a Ritz, seemed to be speaking happily to the cracker, "We are who we think we are."

"That's right, honey, and I think I'm too old for your brother's revolution."

Merle Junior stared at Bob for a long moment then maneuvered the triple-decker back to his mouth. Before taking another bite, he said, "You owe me a story."

Bob nodded, chewing down a sizable hunk of his own sandwich. He took a swig of milk, swallowed, used his own napkin, and then said, "This was back before the beginning of my career. I wasn't cutting it at Second City. Been there a little while, got a few laughs, but nothing consistent and nothing special. There was some concern that Buck's kid brother was turning out to be an untalented favor, that I was taking up a performance slot that should go to someone with real potential."

Perri wiped her lips with a napkin daintily, her feet swinging, quietly kicking the porch table. "I think you have potential, Uncle Bob."

"Thank you, bubalah."

"You are very welcome," she smiled at him. "Please continue your story."

Bob chuckled, and then did what she asked. "This one night was more or less my last shot. We had this improv — that is a form of comedy, bubalah— and I was supposed to run with a particular scene, and I forgot the thread. Couldn't remember my part. My line came up, and I just blurted something out, thinking, 'That's it, I'm toast.'

"And then, snatching me from just totally dying onstage, there it was, one single laugh," Bob said, smiling. "One sincere, real laugh."

He glanced at Merle Junior who sat with his sandwich in his hand, forgotten, jelly finally making a break for it onto the porch table.

Bob's face lit up, in performance mode. "And it was that one laugh from the audience that made all the difference. I said something else. That laugh came again, and brought friends. One of the cast members responded, picking up on this new direction, so I kept riffing. That laugh led a growing wave as the entire audience caught on to where we were going, and I somehow brought the house down. Roaring laughter, huge applause at the end. It became my first signature bit."

Perri's enthusiasm broke in. "I knew you could do

it!" This was exactly what Mary Angeline used to say to the little girl every time she planted a seed or watered a plant well. Delivered exactly in Mary Angeline's cadence.

Bob looked at her smiling face in wonder, savoring the oh-so-brief visitation of his wife's essence; those embers glowed bright momentarily, and then he nodded and continued. "All because of a woman who would soon tell me her name was Mary Angeline."

Perri clapped. "Aunt Mary!"

Bob would have bought that girl a house right then if she asked. He turned to her brother. "So is she righteous? Hell yeah, brother."

Merle Jr. nodded his approval. "Was that the Buttley Burgers bit?"

"No, Buttley came a little later that season—"

"Was it the one that goes, 'Sir, I love this woman even if she is your wife. I'll give you $5.38'?"

Bob laughed a little through his nose. "Yeah, that's it."

"I have it on my hard drive," Merle said, and then, with his mouth full, he said, "Bootleg. Sorry."

"Can't get it any other way, I believe. Wish I could find a clip of that actual performance."

"I'll work on it for you."

Now it was Bob's turn to stare, sandwich forgotten. "Is that even possible?"

"Back then, Harry 'Mac' McIntosh filmed Second City almost every night."

"Yeah," Bob said. "We would study them to see what was working."

"Remember the boxed set? Supposedly that didn't even scratch the surface of what he had, and a lot of the rest has found its way online, so it is worth looking."

"I remember Harry," Bob smiled. "Eventually he DP'd for us on *Jail Broken*. Is he still working?"

"Dead. Prostate cancer. Last year. They discovered it early, too. Used to treat that easily in this country."

"Used to treat a lot of things easily," Bob agreed. "Bastards."

"Language, young man," Perri admonished, sounding a lot like a tiny sheriff.

"My apologies, Perri, I am unfit to be in your presence," Bob bowed.

Perri giggled and danced in her chair, reaching for her last Ritz, quite delighted with the world.

Bob was glad to see someone was.

Merle Jr. continued. "His work is still out there. Tons of Second City stuff. I'll listen for the one laugh."

Bob nodded at the kid, "That's what I do every night."

Chapter 21

LATER, AFTER FINISHING THE rest of the gutters and watering every plant on Bob's property, his favorite guests departed, Perri holding Merle Junior's hand and swinging his arm. The comedian considered dinner options. "Cheerios with blueberries or Cheerios without them, that is the question."

He glanced at Steve, but no sage advice was forthcoming.

"With blueberries it is," he decided, and opened the fridge where he found no such fruity delights. "Alas, the motion has been vetoed."

As he took out the milk, cereal, bowl, and spoon required of this culinary feast, a delightful bebopping sound came from the living room.

Bob grinned at Steve. "Only two urchins in the whole entire world send me that sound. Come on, Steve, it's Suzie-Kalloozie and RobbaDobba! Let's sneak up on them."

Bob grabbed his phone, now alive with the incoming FaceTime call. He set it up so once he slid right to connect, the kids would see a close up of Steve, as if he had answered. "They're gonna love this, Steve. Just stay right their, buddy."

He accepted the call, expecting to hear familiar high-pitched squeals of delight.

Instead, what exploded from the phone were cheers and laughter and applause so loud that Steve bolted from the room. Bob turned the phone, looked at the screen and dropped it. Was the phone malfunctioning? What was writhing around onscreen? Where were the kids? Had they pranked him while he was pranking them? He lifted the screen to his face, and the cheers soared to a roar of approval.

And then the chanting began.

"BOB! BOB! BOB! BOB!"

He looked closer. It was a wall of ... faces.

It slowly dawned at him that these were ... fans.

Long unused muscle memory kicked in and Bob's signature smirk tugged his features to the right as he tilted his head slightly to the left.

The crowd recognized the move from a dozen hit comedies and lost their minds.

Bob laughed, thinking, where are my grandkids? How did they set this up? Maybe it was their school's PTA fundraiser? If so, when are they coming onscreen?

"Suzie-Kalloozie! RobbaDobba! Where are you crazy kids?" Bob spoke over the cheers, searching the crowd for his beloved nuggets.

Then Winston Miller stepped into the foreground wearing a "WE MISS BOB" T-shirt over his shirt and tie. "Bob Murphy, everyone! Finally, we make contact with The All-Time Greatest!"

Whatwhatwhatwhat? Bob's mind raced. Miller? He had only told Jeremy he would think about it ... Damnit, the kid had misunderstood him. Or jumped to conclusions. Or sold him out. He told himself to hang up. Just hang up... on at least a hundred very excited fans and potentially millions more watching on television? Pissed as he was, he owed them more than that.

"Winston, you mischievous chimp you, what are all you crazy maniacs doing?"

The crowds' laughter drowned out Winston's response. He held up a hand to get some control back, and then spoke for all of them. "We all have missed you so much, Bob, and we've been trying to get in touch just to make sure you are okay and to make sure you know we all love you." He turned to the audience. "Isn't that right?"

The crowd roared.

Bob made his smile scrunch up like they were all in on some delightful hijinks together. Inside, his thoughts about Miller had a very different tone.

The crowd applauded wildly for this equally well-known expression.

Miller held up that hand again, the jerk silencing the real people. "We've been told you won't come on television anymore."

"That's because it's true, Winnie," Bob said before he could stop himself. Don't be rude to the fans, he admonished himself, and then countered himself with a reminder that Miller was not a fan, he was an incubus using Bob for his own pleasure.

Miller smiled an empty LA smile. "Are you okay? Your health—"

Bob blinked consciously and offered the pop culture pimp a mocking smile, both moves he made famous while facing down a giant stone possessed former President in *Monster Cops*. "I'm as okay as any of us are, Winston. Thanks for asking."

"You were the funniest, most outspoken voice we

ever had, Bob," Winston slipped into interview mode. "*Monster Cops*, which is being reissued this week in a deluxe package, took on old-time delusions about the so-called Washington elite. *Jail Broken* was hilarious and still spoke about the then-alleged racism in our criminal justice system. Between the gags, *Our Only Boat* commented on climate change — remember the climate change fad, everyone?"

The crowd went wild.

"Remember the Florida Keys?" Bob shot back though no one could hear him. *Old-time delusions? Then-alleged? Remember climate change?* He needed to get out of the trap this soulless pariah had sprung on him—

Winston again quieted the crowd. "All that noise has long since been resolved, God Bless America. What do you do these days, Bob?"

Bob heard his words take on an edge he didn't intend to use out loud. "I stay home, Winston. I talk to people face-to-face, and I listen, really listen to their views whether I agree or not. It is called conversation — remember that fad? I shop at independently owned stores. I mind my own business. What I don't do any longer is contribute to financing, condoning, or being complicit in the madness."

The crowd roared.

Winston let them have their moment, then leaned in close to the camera, as if he were whispering to the comedian. "You used to do that gloriously, on an international stage. What happened, Bob? Did the Powers That Be get to you? Did the world hurt you?"

This leech wanted Bob to give him an Oprah moment, an Emmy segment. He was pushing Bob to break down and commiserate about Mary Angeline. "I just stopped, Winston."

"But making us laugh, and making us think, that's your job. Coming on shows like this, that's your job."

"Well, Winston, if coming on your show is my job, then I'm calling out sick. Maybe more people should do that." Bob hit the red phone icon, ending the intrusion. He stormed into his bedroom, not even knowing why until he started talking to the portrait, something he hadn't done in months.

"Can you believe him? Thinking he had a right to discuss you! He can't pimp a person's pain like that!

"Hopefully, he'll have a harder time getting guests after this stunt! That slime thought I'd discuss *you* with *him*? Really?"

He looked up at the silent, calming portrait. After a few minutes, he sat on the bed. "That just wasn't right. Only the kids use FaceTime ... with ... me. He found out and cloned it!"

Bob lay back and kept staring up at the only one who had ever made jerks tolerable. "To defile the kids' privacy ... our special time ... that's just low...."

His gaze continued, long after her smile slowed his pulse, calmed his anger. Finally, his eyelids lowered. "We showed that ... creep...."

Chapter 22

BOB AWOKE PAST DINNERTIME. He fed the dog, but didn't eat himself — the Miller call had spoiled his appetite. Instead, he scrubbed dishes from the afternoon with fervor, making sure each sparkled before putting it in the dishwasher. Then the kitchen counters and porch table were cleaned with equal energy, and Steve's bowl was made to all but glow. Floors were swept and mopped despite the cleaning lady having visited just a few days earlier, and all the garbage containers were emptied, relined, and the bags taken out to the bins until tomorrow morning's ride.

Still not hungry, Bob dumped himself onto the couch and hit the remotes.

"... be sure to see an exclusive tonight on Miller Time—"

Click.

"...the reclusive comedy icon has broken his long silence—"

CLICK.

"Bob Murphy is back, folks—"

CLICK!

Bob turned off the television, slammed the remote down on the couch. He leapt to his feet, stormed around the house. "Why did I even pick up the phone, Steve?"

Steve had no answer.

"Did it say the kids' names? I thought so, but it couldn't have. And that music, I thought that was just for the kids, but maybe that's just the FaceTime ringtone. I don't know social media that well." He tossed the phone onto the couch near the remotes.

Steve gazed up at him with soulful brown eyes.

"Yeah, bro, we both have to up our tech game."

Bob and Steve stomped around the house for a long while, eventually slowing to an amble, and then finally wandering over to the bookshelves in the small library at the end of the hall. "Enough with the world for tonight. You with me?"

The dog was most certainly with him. Right at his ankles.

Bob perused shelves full of well-thumbed paperbacks he had owned for decades. "What we need is some solid distraction from a good ol' Texas boy. Which will it be, Robert E. Howard or Michael Moorcock?"

Steve inclined his head slightly to the right.

"An evening with Elric of Melniboné it is."

And in this way, with both the phone and the television off, Bob and Steve were completely unaware of what had been unleashed.

Chapter 23

PREDAWN, BOB PACKED THE garbage in the bike baskets, grabbed his wallet, a bottle of water, his house keys....

"Where's the damned phone?"

He and Steve looked everywhere, until he remembered shutting it off and tossing it onto the couch. When he turned the phone back on, the damn thing nearly vibrated out of his hand as message after message uploaded. Bob didn't do social media, so these were all voicemails.

Percy from the barbershop said, "Good job, Bob! For you, we gonna stay closed today."

Merle, Jr. said, "Great line. So many kids listened they had to close the school. That's hilarious."

A woman from the movie company whispered, "Mr. Murphy, we're with you. So many of us are calling out, too."

"This is Florena, we closed the theater in solidarity."

Jeremy was positively joyous. "Can you believe the overnight numbers? I don't know why you decided to go ahead on your own, but you made me look like a genius, so thank you! Your clip is going ridiculously viral. On YouTube, it already has over a million hits. In a few hours! Your rallying cry is being shared everywhere, even on National News! And people are following your advice."

Bob asked no one, "What advice?"

He grabbed the taped-up television remote, clicked on National News.

Some morning talking head was saying, "We haven't seen a populist movement like this since the Trump years. Businesses are finding they can't open their doors for lack of staff, and corporations are reporting record absences, all because of a few words from a long retired comedian."

Her counterpart adjusted his glasses pompously, countering, "Well, of course, the impetus was there among the Easily Hysterical, broiling underneath their daily lives, waiting for just one more thing to push them needlessly over the edge. All Murphy did was nudge the liberals into the tantrums they love to throw." He seemed to review his statement, and concern crossed his jowly face. He hurried to add, "Of course this is reckless and unacceptable."

A third sucked his teeth, then said, "Record numbers staying home. We barely have a skeleton crew here at the station. And these unpatriotic stats keep climbing. It's more than a nudge. This just might be treason."

"Treason!" Bob stood in the middle of his living room stunned. "What did I say?"

Chapter 24

BY MIDDAY, "BREAKING NEWS" anchors on every station —even the illegal ones— were reporting what Bob could only process as lunacy. According to the various reports, somewhere between 20 and 25 percent of the workforce had "called out sick" from their jobs, and all the anchors were attributing the mass absences to one sentence Bob had uttered off the cuff.

"Well, Winston, if coming on your show is my job, then I'm calling out sick. Maybe more people should do that."

They played the clip over and over, and reports grew of more and more people leaving work, "calling out sick" for their afternoon and night shifts, and "calling out sick" in advance for tomorrow.

"Well, Winston, if coming on your show is my job, then I'm calling out sick. Maybe more people should do that."

"What the hell did I do, Steve?"

Steve didn't know.

Neither did Bob.

The garbage remained in the bike baskets and the morning dishes didn't get done — in fact, nothing got done as the two of them watched dumbfounded as the numbers of participants in "The Bob Murphy National Sick Out" continued to climb.

Chapter 25

NATIONAL NEWS ANCHORS STRUGGLED to make some sense of the effects of Bob's TV appearance.

"Online rentals of Bob Murphy films have surged, so perhaps his fans aren't boycotting all of the economy," one self-impressed anchor reported with a smirk. "And President Statler suspects the comedian's sagging finances might be behind his un-American war cry, tweeting, 'Now we know what is behind all this; it is a stunt to boost Murphy's bank account. Pitiful.'"

Joining Bob and Steve on the couch, Merle, Jr. barked a sardonic laugh. "You just got smacked by a moron."

Murphy chuckled. "Yeah, well, His Dimness may have just given all of us an out," he said, thumbing his phone to life.

After searching without success, he handed it to the teenager. "Where is my Twitter account?"

Merle Jr. snorted another laugh, found the app, opened it, found Bo's tweet and hit "reply".

Bob thanked him, and then sent a series of tweets.

> *Replying to @RealPresidentStatler*
> *My finances are in great shape, Bo,*
> *thanks for the concern. Ask Miller how*
> *this happened.*

Replying to @RealPresidentStatler
But, if you want, POTUS, my man, I'd
love to have you over to the house.

Replying to @RealPresidentStatler
We could grill up some burgers, have
some cold brews, and talk this out.

Replying to @RealPresidentStatler
I know I would love that. I suspect
America would love that. I hope you
will, too.

Replying to @RealPresidentStatler
So POTUS Bo, come on over. Tweet
back and let me know if you want
cheese on them burgers.

Almost immediately a response appeared.

Replying to @BobMurphy
The President represents True
Americans; POTUS will not be going
anywhere near you for burgers.

Merle Junior's laughter sounded like muffled machine gun fire. Once he regained his composure, he shook his head. "Statler 2, Murphy 0."

"Maybe not," Bob said, staring open-mouthed at his phone He held it up so the kid could see.

Bob's screen was almost a blur as thousands retweeted Statler's message with comments such as:

@fakeID Replying to @
RealPresidentStatler Anyone who

rejects a backyard invite is no True
American. #BurgersAmAmerica

@CrankCase Replying to @

RealPresidentStatler Bo's showing his
true colors and they aren't red, white,
and blue. #FakeAmerican

@JustinBurb Replying to @
RealPresidentStatler C'mon Bo,
grab a burger and beer with
Bob. Maybe you two can finally
reunite this shattered country.
#That'sWhataRealPrezWouldDo

Merle Jr. studied the responses carefully. Finally, he looked up and said, "This is kind of awesome."

Bob shook his head. "All I did was end an unwanted FaceTime call."

Merle Jr. waved away Bob's humility. "All Obama did was insult Trump."

"Uh oh," Bob said.

Merle Jr. smiled, "Now you begin to glimpse the truth. Only one question remains."

"And that is?"

"How soon will they crush you?"

Chapter 26

BEFORE BOB REALLY UNDERSTOOD what was happening, the end had begun.

By the afternoon, things turned dangerous. Bob's former comedy partner, the ever-acerbic Lionel Jackson, showed up at a Freedom Processing Center outside of Hattiesburg, Mississippi, with the media in tow, and went off live on television.

In truth, Lionel had been patient on this longer than Bob thought was possible for him. His former partner had a penchant for yelling first and thinking whether he should have later.

Civil rights protections had long been under siege, first with the banning of illegal aliens, and then brown people of all nationalities were made subject to "extreme vetting" if they wished to emigrate, which became so extreme most nonwhites stopped applying for visas or green cards to America and chose Canada, Australia, England and Ireland instead.

Then the True American Safety Enforcement (TASE) agency was created to the arrest, prosecute, and deport even American-born minorities. Legal challenges exploded and the government's response was to create Freedom Processing Centers where "questionable Americans" could be held "safely" while inconsistencies with the law and True American efforts to keep the country "safe" (pronounced "white") were "being resolved."

The camps grew, coincidentally on enormous farmlands where detainees were put to work growing their own food and making their own clothes, a small percentage of which they were actually allowed to keep.

All of this started on what became known as True Americans Day, now a national holiday complete with greeting cards and Red, White, and Blue Sales days.

When President Bo signed all of these bills into law, he also launched, via executive order, a program called True Americans Registration. This was a protection for all adult citizens that called for the implanting of a True American Safety Tracker into the neck of each righteous resident "to keep them out of harm's way."

"True Americans will never again find themselves at the mercy of the growing Minority, Gay, Terrorist Complex which threatens our nation's future. Once True Americans are gifted with the trackers, they will never be vulnerable to such threats again because the full power of the American military will immediately rush to their aid," Statler proclaimed, loosening the collar of his pressed white shirt and accepting his own tracker injection in the Oval Office, and the source of Merle Junior's conspiracy theory.

True American Registration started with our poorest citizens, "the ones most in need of our protections," Bo declared. The injection program was meant to climb through the economic strata of the nation until everyone was "protected" but had yet to find its way beyond working class and minority neighborhoods.

Instead, processing centers became "registration points" as well, so, if some ACLU lawyer forced the government to free a few of the processing center registrants, they would be traceable. Easier to find and charge with the next crime.

And Lionel Jackson was standing right in front of one of those nightmare camps about to call out the government on all of it.

Bob swallowed, made the sign of the cross, and prayed.

Chapter 27

THE CAMERAS CLOSED IN on Lionel. His close cropped hair was more gray now, but that trademark scowl still started at his furiously furrowed brows, shot fiery intolerance from his always alert eyes, and scrunched one side of his nose and mouth up in a snarl that had defined his comedic outrage, offsetting Bob's more amiable wiseass persona. Each complimented the other's performance style, the mix proving irresistible to millions. Together they enjoyed the biggest comedy success of their careers.

And then Bo stranded Mary Angeline, and everything ended.

Bob watched his all-time favorite comedian approach the microphones and thought about Lionel's patience. And he had been patient, but not silent. His old partner had never been silent on anything that bothered him in his entire life. He made political and cultural horrors a central focus of his stand-up shows. Lionel could do 60 minutes on a dozen controversial topics and keep audiences howling throughout his sold-out comedy tours. And he did, until the Shadow Lopez Incident ended live comedy for all.

Shadow Lopez was one of their contemporaries, quick and daring, irreverent and funny as hell. He was headlining the Latinos of Laughter Tour and was five minutes into a performance that was broadcast live on HBO from a sold out Madison Square Garden in NYC. Shadow was riffing mercilessly on the incompetency of the president when a shot rang out and Lopez's head exploded on international television.

Chaos ensued. The crowd stampeded for the exits. Hundreds were injured.

HBO cut immediately to calmer entertainment, repeating a *Game of Thrones* episode.

To twist the knife, the president tweeted his "condolences."

> @RealPresidentStatler: We just witnessed that free speech isn't free. #TrueAmerica #ResponsiblyFree

> @RealPresidentStatler: These are unsafe times. True Americans must register and get trackers. #RememberShadowLopez

Bo used the assassination as a promotional tool for one of his pet projects. No other efforts were made to bring Shadow Lopez' killer to justice.

The message was loud and clear.

Cutting edge comedy ended. No venue would book "dangerous" comedians.

Comics who did continue subsisted on touring small clubs equipped with big metal detectors, focusing on safer comedic terrain like airplane food, shopping lists and relationship jokes.

America forgot how to laugh at itself.

Onscreen, Lionel Jackson was in angry performance mode. "My man Bobby is telling everyone to stay home. Not me. I asked you all to come out here because we've been home long enough. Today, I'm speaking up, too."

Bob rose slowly from the couch. "Oh no," he murmured.

Lionel started in, taking a step to the right or left as he would during his act, but staying in front of the cameras like the pro he was. "The president of these not so United States is laying out some lies about this prison right here behind me! He says: 'These Freedom Processing Centers are just screening for True Americans.' That's some damn bullshit. And he says, 'The Islamic religious are not being held, Muslim extremists are.' That's some bullshit right there, too, because my cousin Monique is being held up in here and she is one mouse-quiet, rug-kneeling, Allah-praying honey of a girl. I've seen her goodness. Does the prez care? Hell no! Bo also says, 'All religions are protected under the Constitution, including Islam.' If that is so, why is Monique and her whole Muslim community living in this prison camp for damn near a year?"

A reporter asked, "Why do you see this Freedom Processing Center as a prison?"

"Because Muslims check in but they don't check out."

Another reporter said, "President Statler claims the government is just being thorough, that he would rather be thorough than dead."

He shot back, "Can you point to a single criminal incident that can be traced to these people right here the government is illegally holding in this prison?"

Suddenly a uniformed officer walked up to the comedy legend. "No, because we've prevented all that potential death and destruction they would have caused. You're welcome."

Lionel was not having it. "Don't be obtuse. I mean before they were detained! Not so much as a parking ticket! Not even a library late fee for my True American cousin Monique!"

"She must have done something," the uniformed man said. "True Americans don't get arrested."

Lionel wasn't having any of that either. "Get outta my face, Sergeant Klansman!"

"Please, Lionel," Bob said to the television, "just walk away, buddy."

Onscreen, the officer took a step toward Lionel. "You need to remove yourself from this government facility, Lionel Jackson, because you are trespassing."

"I pay taxes, this is a government facility my taxes help finance, so trespassing my ass."

Chaos erupted as additional soldiers rushed Lionel from all sides, shouting "Gun!" and "Do not resist!" Even before Lionel could move a muscle, Bob's friend and former partner was swallowed in a sea of green-clad men. Then one of the soldiers jammed a hand into the camera, and the feed was cut.

An anchor appeared onscreen. "That was coming to you live from a Freedom Processing Center right outside Hattiesburg, Mississippi, where once-famous comedian Lionel Jackson just provoked a showdown with the U.S. government, possibly brandishing a weapon, and lost."

"That's not what he did," Bob shouted as he speed dialed Jeremy. It went to voicemail. "Jeremy! We need to help Lionel! Call me!"

Merle Jr. came bursting through the unlocked door with his little sister. "Take care of Steve, Perri," he said, and then turned to the bewildered comedian. "Are you nuts, Bob? You need to be barricaded in right now," the teen scolded, locking the front door.

Bob noticed his purple hair was jet black now. And all of his piercings were empty. And he was wearing a patrol uniform like his father's.

"The Sheriff deputized me to help you," the kid explained. "He's already got his troops stationed around your property but needs you to stay inside, with all your doors and windows locked, shades down and curtains drawn."

Bob instinctively went toward the kitchen window. "What the hell are you talking about?"

Merle Jr. blocked him. "We got word that news trucks were coming. Pop has them blocked off about two miles down, but they are demanding access. They want to be here when TASE arrives to crush you. Pop is praying reinforcements from County arrive before the Nazis do."

Bob and Merle Jr. went around the house locking doors and windows, and drawing shades and curtains, until everything was secured and nerve-racking.

The comedian asked no one in particular, "How did this happen?"

"Wonders of modern tech," the kid said, "You crack wise once, and before you know it your world is on fire. This is your reality now; you're the outlaw of the week."

Bob smirked, "At least it is just this week."

"You won't survive three days."

"Thanks for giving me the benefit of doubt."

Perri's voice whispered from behind a big storybook she was reading to Steve all cuddled in the corner of the couch. "There is no benefit to doubt."

Merle Jr. smiled. "You're so smart, Perri. Maybe you should teach this guy."

Chapter 28

WHILE WAITING FOR DRAMA to develop at Bob's house, National News was paneling the entire "Bob Murphy Uprising" into a national security crisis. As Bob and the siblings watched on the kitchen TV, Bling kept pulling her surprisingly less-than-spectacular hair around her unusually pale complexion as she spoke. "Sources are now suggesting that it may have been Murphy who hacked into Miller's show to launch his failed revolution."

"I didn't hack in, he called me," Bob argued from the sink where he was rewashing clean dishes. "You idiot!"

Perri, at the kitchen table, made an "O" face.

"I apologize for my language, bubalah," Bob said.

The junior sheriff was more edgy than usual. "Enough with the TV talking heads," he muttered. "When does the media show up? It will be harder for TASE to do what it does while they are being filmed."

"Tell your father that," Bob smirked mirthlessly.

"He doesn't understand," Merle Jr. said. "He thinks this is keeping the peace."

The sound of cars rolling onto Bob's property alarmed them.

Perri announced happily, "Ready or not, here comes company!"

Merle Jr. hurried to the window. "TASE agents, to be sure," he fretted.

Bob peeked out in a much meeker fashion, and then smiled. "Not TASErs," he said, "that line of limos is Hollywood riding to the rescue."

"You think actor friends can help?"

"Nope, but these people might."

Three limos drove past them to the back of the house. Another stopped by the house's entrance, others swung in front of it forming an expensive blockade. The last vehicle to turn onto Bob's property was not a limo but a flatbed truck with a huge, billboard-sized version of the *Monster Cops* movie poster made of super thick cardboard. The truck swung onto Bob's lawn so the movie poster blowup would serve as a backdrop for the young exec climbing out of the last limo.

Bob smiled at seeing his nemesis direct the tech crew to where he wanted the podium and microphone set up. "Jeremy, I retract everything I ever said about you and your dubious family tree," Bob murmured.

Merle Jr. was more interested in the suits emerging from the other cars. "Who are they?"

"They, my young friend, are members of what looks like an entire law office," Bob said.

"What clown would send attorneys to a raid by a federal law enforcement agency?"

"The clown who runs their firm, my son Jackson."

Now it was Merle Junior's turn to make an "O" face.

Chapter 29

JACKSON ROBIN PRYOR MURPHY was not playing around. Before saying hello to his father, the founder and CEO of Murphy, Murphy & Hicks requested strategic repositioning for some of Sheriff Merle's men, launched a search of his father's premises with drug-sniffing dogs by private security specialists he had brought with him, and then organized a wall of lawyers, each armed with motions and writs and whatever else lawyers arm themselves with in defense of their clients, of which Bob was their first and foremost.

"Dogs, son?" Bob said in greeting.

"Preventive defense, Pop," Jackson said, hugging his father and kissing him on the cheek. "We received word that TASE are coming, and we've been tipped they are going to try doing to you what they pulled with Uncle Lionel yesterday."

"You saw the news? Why aren't you there getting him released?"

"Willie is already there filing motions on his behalf. My priority is you, Pop."

"What's the big deal? I was rude to a talk show host—"

Jackson looked to Merle Jr. "You couldn't make him understand, officer?"

Merle Jr. reddened a little at the assumed authority

but did not correct Jackson. "The facts do not register with this dreamer."

Jackson nodded, "You got his number."

Bob waved a hand in dismissal. "What, the people calling out sick? That's Jeremy hyping the new Blu-Ray, Jackie. Look at him out there; it's a publicity stunt."

"Dad—"

"That kid's gonna get a promotion over this," Bob chuckled. "Did he put you up to bringing all these guys over? Are they actors? Should I fire up the grill?"

"Dad, sit—"

Bob's smile seemed forced now. "Not your usual style, counselor."

"Dad, I need you to sit down."

"You shoulda brought the kids. They'd love all this exciting goofiness—"

"Dad! Your grandchildren are in hiding."

Bob stopped cold.

"I had Veronica take them way off the radar."

Bob's voice was quiet now. "What are you talking about?"

"This is real serious trouble, Pop," Jackson said, moving his head so he was eye-to-eye with his father. "We don't understand it; no one has seen numbers like this in decades. But this is real; your words hit a nerve. As a result the 'sick out' is happening across the country. You caused a rebellion."

"I meant ... other guests...."

"That doesn't matter now," Jackson moved his father to a seat. "The public thinks you meant them, and, whether out of loyalty to you or just sheer frustration, people started calling out from work. Miller's people pimped the clip of your appearance to every digital, television, cable, and social media platform in the country. Fans took it viral. Then all the news outlets made it their lead, and clips of those shows also went viral — insane numbers — which kicked Miller's actual ratings into the stratosphere, and fans posted the actual clip of you on FaceTime with him on their social media pages and YouTube channels. Your appearance has the highest saturation rates ever."

"But I'm a has been...."

"The numbers argue the opposite; millions of people stayed home because you suggested it."

"Then why is Jeremy out there with a damn movie billboard?"

"Pop, you need to understand that it doesn't matter how he's trying to spin this, or what you meant, or what the actual facts are; every media outlet in the country is attributing the kneecapping of our economy to your words, and they are doing it on around the clock," Jackson insisted. "Every. Media. Outlet."

"Then Jeremy better deliver the spin of the century."

"To whom? The sheriff won't let the media anywhere near this place, and without them—"

Merle Jr. finished the sentence for him. "TASE will rip us all apart."

Jackson turned to face the kid. "Not with all my lawyers out there."

Bob added, "Not with kids here."

"Rich people," Merle snorted as he walked out.

Chapter 30

JEREMY HAD THE PODIUM and microphone set up in front the 20-foot *Monster Cops* billboard. He took a quick sip of water (actually straight vodka), swallowed, and spoke to the sheriff who stood before him arms folded, mirror shades in place, a thin slit of a frown suggesting the young man had lost his argument before a word was said.

"We'll set up the media right over there," Jeremy tried.

"We will do no such thing."

"The media is essential to the peaceful resolution of this situation, sir," Jeremy insisted.

"In my long years of law enforcement experience, son, the circus never helped anyone but themselves."

"I must insist on freedom of the press."

"The revolution will not be televised today, boy, not so you can resell some old movie for my neighbor."

Jeremy called out. "Louie drive the billboard down to the press and inform them that all efforts to get local law enforcement to recognize foundational freedoms are being ignored."

Louie climbed into the truck.

Sheriff Merle called out. "Officer Atkins, follow that truck about four blocks and then pull it over and keep it there."

"Don't stop, Lou!"

"If Lou doesn't stop, shoot out the truck's tires, Officer Atkins," the sheriff smiled, yellow smoker's teeth flashing. "And if Louie here gets out and runs, you are to shoot him in the ass. If he tries to get up, you are to shoot him in the ass again."

Lou called out from the truck, "See you in four blocks, Officer Atkins."

"Louie!"

"Sorry, Jeremy, my wife likes this ass too much," Louie grinned and then drove the billboard off the property.

Sheriff Merle smirked. "Well, that's settled."

Jeremy took another swig of 80-proof water. "Sheriff, without the media here recording everything, TASE will frame my client like they did his old partner just yesterday."

"I have jurisdiction, and these lawyer fellas will have a word or two to say about your client's rights."

From behind his father, Merle Jr. spoke, "None of that will make a difference to TASE, Dad."

Sheriff Merle turned in surprise. "Did you just called me—"

"No time for that, Pop—"

"'Pop' too! This is a banner day!"

Merle Jr. let an edge into his voice. "We are running out of time."

Jeremy stepped between father and son. "Sheriff, TASE believe they are about to confront a terrorist who has caused national damage to the economy and the daily lives of so-called True Americans. Local police and out of state lawyers cannot compete with their faith in their own interpretation of the facts."

"Son, I don't expect you to understand professional courtesy—"

Jeremy screamed, "Are you even listening to me?"

Merle, Jr. demanded, "Pop, TASE will not respect your authority here."

The sheriff, annoyed now, slashed an arm across the space between the three of them. "This conversation is over." He turned and strode to his men.

Merle Jr. turned to Jeremy, "We have go to Plan B."

Jeremy, lost and a little drunk, shook his head. "What's Plan B?"

"We take Bob to the media."

Chapter 31

JACKSON FOLLOWED HIS FATHER around the house as Bob cleaned already spotless furniture. Perri, blissfully unconcerned by all the adult drama, snuck Steve's bowls out of the dishwasher and gave the dog some water and food.

Merle Jr. burst in and snapped her up dog food bag and all. "Sorry Perri, but we have to go right now!"

"Where, Merle? It is not even dinner time yet."

"We can't wait for dinner time, honey, Daddy's going to have a lot of police work to do out there and we need to be elsewhere, all of us."

Jeremy came in behind Merle Jr. and continued over to Bob and Jackson. "The kid's right. We need to go now. TASE is coming to arrest you for terroristic activity."

"That is not what happened," Bob fumed.

"So go out there and tell them the truth," Jackson challenged.

"No, no, no!" Jeremy waved his hands before them. "Wrong idea. Bad idea. We need—"

Merle Jr., packing up Perri's backpack, called over, interrupting the showbiz whiz. "To take one of the cars in the back and drive down to the media. You can have your say there."

Bob held up his hands as if they were stop signs.

"Hey, I've already said too much. That's how all this started."

Jackson pressed. "People are counting on you, Pop."

Bob shook his head. "People are amused by me, not the same as being the Reverend Doctor King, buddy."

Merle Jr. and Perri joined Jeremy and Jackson, forming a loose circle around Bob. Merle Jr. adding, "Chaplin amused people with *The Great Dictator* in 1940, and at the same time he helped them see what Hitler really was."

Bob nodded at the teen. "Good movie. Brilliant."

Jackson lifted the BluRay of *Monster Cops*. "So was your work."

Bob looked up. "I thought you had never seen my work."

"All of them, several times."

Bob offered a pleased, "Huh." He thought for a minute, turned back to Merle Jr., "Bo isn't Hitler."

Merle Jr. retorted, "Every society gets the kind of criminal it deserves."

Now Jackson was pleased. "Robert Kennedy. Impressive."

"And yet we are still here when we should be gone," Merle Jr. shook his head.

"Off to see the media? I pass," Bob said, returning his attention to cleaning an immaculate counter.

Jeremy pleaded, "This place is not safe—"

"For any of us," Merle Jr. interrupted, his arm lifting Perri.

"Point taken," Bob said, blowing Perri a kiss. "You guys should go. Take the car in the back."

Merle Jr. seemed shocked. "And what are you going to do?"

Bob smiled first at the boy and then at the rest of them. "Keep my word." When they didn't seem to understand he spread his arms as if to encompass the house. "I said I was staying home, and that's what I'm going to do."

Jackson understood. "Why aren't you working, Dad?"

Bob cleaned another clean surface. "You better go," he murmured. "You all said it isn't safe. Go."

"It's because of Mom, right? Your career was based on making her laugh. You developed all that great comedy to amuse her first," he said. "Dad, I was there. You don't think I remember?"

Bob said nothing.

"And then she died, and you decided the public died, too. So instead of using the incredible gifts Mom confirmed were yours for 30 years, you cooked burgers at Little League games and limited your travels to local Mom and Pop stores in town?"

Bob looked at Jackson, then away.

"Mom shows you how talented you are for 30 years, and once she's gone, you don't believe her anymore?"

Bob walked toward his bedroom. "Good seeing you, son. Take these kids to meet yours, please."

Jackson stormed after him. "I want to know why you are wasting your days confined to this small town!"

Bob spun back to face his son. "Because Mom loved it! All of it! Little League. The shops. Being treated like regular people in town. And especially this house. That's all I have left of her. Who are you to ask me to give what remains of the woman I loved?"

Bob walked into his bedroom and began adjusting up a perfectly made bed. Jackson followed, jolting to a his mother's stuff still exactly where it was the day Bob rushed her to the hospital.

His father wandered the slightly stuffy room in their awkward silence, flattening the doily on Mary Angeline's dresser, pressing down the corner that always curled up. He touched her statue of the Blessed Mother, chipped and scarred from years of Jackson as a boy running in and bouncing off the furniture, knocking her over countless times.

When Jackson saw the portrait everything stopped for a long moment. When he spoke, it was reverently. "I haven't seen this in ... years.... She was so...."

"Yeah. She was."

Silence reclaimed the room, awkward and painful for both.

Finally, Jackson spoke. "You really started something when you FaceTimed--"

"Miller FaceTimed me. It was a setup."

"Dad, you took the call."

"I thought it was Suzie and Robbie. No one else FaceTimes me."

"Still, you said what you said, and started some sort of crazy movement."

"Wasn't my plan. I don't want any of them getting hurt."

"Did you mean what you said?"

"I didn't think it would start all this, but yeah, I meant it. I meant people shouldn't just blindly go along with Miller or any of the other TV mouthpieces, be they celebrities like me, or news anchors, or politicians. People shouldn't just accept other people telling them how to live, or what's right, or how to define what America is. I wanted other guests to blow off Miller, but all the rest of it was in there, too. I just don't want people losing what they do have because I mouthed off."

"But people are following you now, millions of them, because they see themselves in you, just like they always have. Pop, people are fed up with what's going on and they see your words as some kind of answer."

"Tell'em to go listen to your godfather. He was always better at politics than me."

Jackson looked more shocked at this than his mother's belongings. "Dad."

Bob considered his own words, nodding. "That's actually a good idea. Get Lionel to lead them. These millions you're talking about, they loved both of us. Let's get them to join Lionel's protest to get his family out of that damned internment camp, and he'll really fire them up. Go do tha—"

"They imprisoned him too, Dad."

It was as if Jackson had slapped him. "What?"

"Once all this started, Uncle Lionel was the only target that presented himself publicly. What you didn't see on television is them beating him horribly and then dragging him unconscious and bleeding into the camp."

"Bo imprisoned Jackson?"

"Indefinitely."

"On what grounds?"

"Terroristic activity."

Bob Murphy sat on his bed. After awhile, he looked at his son. "What the hell is going on out there?"

"That's what we need to discuss."

Chapter 32

AFTER A QUICK, UNSETTLING discussion, Bob and Jackson rejoined the others who were watching a live, distant shot of the house on National News. Bob glanced at the screen, and then to Jeremy. "The company couldn't send all their top guys to help you?"

Jackson's laugh was joyless. "As soon as this hit, private planes filled the air over LA," he said. "Any executive who thought the press might call for a quote fled the country."

"Do you think Jeremy and I will be enough?"

Jackson sighed. "They will want to see you out there, soon, begging forgiveness, and then on Miller's show, begging forgiveness, and you may even need to appear before Statler himself, bending the knee."

"Doesn't he think so little of me he won't even meet for burgers?"

Jackson leveled a look at his father. "Who do you think is sending TASE?"

Chapter 33

THE PRESIDENT HIMSELF HAD named his specially created "task force" True American Security Enforcement because he wanted a "cool acronym" and thought TASE sounded intimidating. Bob always thought it sounded like a name he and Lionel should have written into *Monster Cops*. After the revelation that Bo had sent TASE after him, Bob's demeanor changed. The combative Bob from the films emerged.

"Really?" His tone was a challenge, not a question. "He wants to play?"

"Oh no," Jackson said.

Bob ignored him. "Merle, call Pop's and tell him I need coffee and donuts for, let's say 50 guests. Send it to where the media is being held, with my compliments."

The kid shrugged. "Should we really offer refreshments to the carnivores who helped propel you into this mess?"

"Hopefully, we'll lower their defenses."

The boy grinned. "Well played." He sauntered off dialing his phone.

Jackson was not amused. "Dad, this is not the time for your hijinks. We're in dangerous waters here."

Bob smiled at his son, a long unlit fire now burning in his eyes. "Not while you have my back."

Jackson raised an eyebrow, a move his father made

famous. It looked better on his son, Bob thought.

"That's a first," Jackson said.

"This whole thing is a first," Bob nodded.

"Dad, if this goes sideways...."

Bob hugged him, whispering, "Jackie, the whole world already has. But with you here, no matter what happens, I'm already better off."

When they separated, Jackson's face changed expression a few times before he nodded. "Dad ... I ... All right. All right. Let's get going."

Bob shook his head, smiling widely. "Go? Jackson, we're already there."

Chapter 34

JACKSON, MERLE, JR., AND Jeremy stared at Bob, confused. Jackson told him, "Dad, we already discussed this. You can't stay here."

"Technically, I won't."

"Excuse me?"

"You say TASE is coming and we should run."

Merle Jr. spoke up. "We should have already."

"What do they want with me?"

Jeremy actually raised his hand before speaking. "They want to charge you with inciting public unrest."

"Actually, everybody stayed home, so I accidentally incited public rest."

Jackson stepped in. "They won't be laughing, they'll be arresting. If you insist on staying, they'll be doing worse."

"I have an idea about that," Bob said. "I'm worried about letting everybody down, right? Because I yapped on FaceTime and said I was staying home. But you all insist I leave. What if we ask everybody's permission? We can FaceTime them and see what they say."

Jackson laughed, pulling his phone from a pocket. "That's not exactly how FaceTime works, Pop, but your idea is almost genius."

"Story of my life," Bob grinned. "Who are you calling?"

"My executive goddess." He hit speed dial, listened a second, and then spoke into the phone, "Dolores? Yes, we're okay. About to get better. I need your team to blow up all my father's social media platforms; announce he's going to on Funbook Live right now."

Bob gave him a quizzical look. "I have social media platforms?"

"You're team has them covered."

"The Cubs?"

"Jokes again." Jackson shook his head, chuckling. "I hired a PR team years ago to keep you current. They work out of my office and have only one client. You have several million followers."

"I have a Funbook page?"

Most people had abandoned Facebook years ago to the political trolls who had ruined it. To salvage his billions, Zuckerberg splintered his baby into several platforms. Facebook for getting into people's faces, Funbook for positive sharing and fan interaction (pronounced promotion), Hobbybook for enthusing over hobbies, Nightbook for online flirting, and so on. Several platforms later, ol' Zuck was a multitrillionaire.

Jackson opened Pop's Funbook account, hit some buttons, and then looked over the phone. "Ready?"

Bob was a little misty.

Jackson, startled, let his finger hover over the record button. "What's wrong, Pop?"

"Despite the TASE-manian devils heading our way, nothing at all," Bob smiled, some of that mist rolling down his cheek. "I'm just thinking of how proud your mom and godfather would be seeing you in action."

Chapter 35

AFTER BOB HAD MADE three hit movies with Lionel Jackson, Mary Angeline gave birth to a boy.

Lionel Jackson came to the hospital with a giant stuffed panda. "See? Black and white, just like us."

Bob hugged him, and then said, "We want you to be his godfather."

Lionel scowled theatrically. "You will do anything to be related to me."

"And we're naming him after you."

"Aw, Hell no! You can't name a white boy Lionel! He'll get beat up in kindergarten!"

Bob was insistent. "We want to do this."

"You name him Lionel, you're painting a target on him. Trust me, I know."

From her bed, Mary Angeline said, "Let's name him Jackson."

Bob looked from his wife to his best friend. "That works for me."

Lionel looked at the little blonde boy in the basinet, and grinned. "We'll tell the other whiteboys to call him Jack, that's a whiteboy name."

Their laughter startled the sleeping infant, who jumped but did not awaken. "He sleeps like a rock," Lionel said, nodding sagely. "He'll do fine in my family."

Chapter 36

JACKSON ADJUSTED HIS IPHONE. "You ready, Pop? Know what you are going to say?"

Bob shrugged, ran his fingers through his hair, improving it not one iota. "I'll think of something."

Jackson paused for a moment, concerned, until his father offered an encouraging wink. He hit the button, counted his father down: three, two, one, and then gave him an index finger indicating "go".

"Hey, everybody. First of all, I am amazed at what you've all been doing. To see news reports about millions of you crazy maniacs independently making the decision to stay home, that's actual American spirit. Somehow, this became like a really relaxed Boston Tea Party, except no one is breaking laws, or inciting violence while a huge statement is being made — so, hey, bravo, you nuts.

"And that's why I'm here talking live on, well, whatever app we're on right now. You see, this big sick out has ticked off Washington, and they're sending some pretty irritable TASE boys to harass me on my own property.

"Don't worry about me, my son has his whole law firm here, but TASE is going to want me to renounce what all of us are doing. Why anyone cares about what I say mystifies me, but they have my good friend and film partner, Lionel Jackson, and his family, in an internment camp. Now, you and I know Lionel is wayyyyy better at getting himself into trouble than he is at getting himself out of it, so here's where I need your help. We want the TASEr–in–Chief to release Lionel and his family. They should release everyone in all those camps, but this is a start. The catch is, the TASE people are probably going to want to arrest me or at least will demand that I leave home for questioning. I don't really trust storm troopers to keep me and mine safe, so it is probably a good idea to be gone when they show up.

"They seem to think forcing me to leave home, under arrest or under duress, will betray all of you and get them a win. But I don't want to betray anyone, so I need your permission.

"Here's what I'm asking: is it cool with all of you if I leave here to stay safe while we try to free Lionel, his family, and all the immorally imprisoned people?"

Suddenly, Bob looked over the top of Jackson's phone to his son. "Hey, is there a comment section below this?"

Jackson nodded.

Bob turned back to the camera. "Okay, there's a comment section below this, and I'm asking you to write a comment either giving me permission to do this or telling me I suck or whatever. Can you do that? I'd really feel better having your support. Okay, I'm going to get off this thing and see how you answer. Thanks. See you soon, hopefully not in handcuffs."

Jackson hit some buttons to finalize, waited for it to go live.

"Anything?" Bob asked nervously.

"Hold on," Jackson said, watching the screen, refreshing, watching some more.

And then he laughed.

Responses were flooding in faster than he could count. He showed his father:

> Responding to @BobMurphy:
>
> **Silly4u**: *Bob, you never need our permission to do anything! We're with you!*
>
> **MikeLovesEggs**: *Go for it, Bob!*
>
> **Stewed**: *TASE sucks! Monster Cops rules! Yes!*
>
> **LisaMcBride455**: *Yes!*
>
> **BillBesser**: *Yep!*
>
> **Tina2Mom**: *We'll help free your friend, Mr. Murphy!*
>
> **JimJimQB10**: *You suck! JK! Go get'em, Murph!*
>
> **DorothyFan**: *Yes, Cutie, absolutely yes!*
>
> **Yennaya**: *Free my Lionel! He's my favorite!*
>
> **FunnyRican**: *Of course you need to go. Want us to go with you?*

PietroLives: *We should march on Washington! These guys play too much!*

CharlesChaun: *You deserve to be thrown in with him, fascist.*

Cindirocks: *A march on Washington might free Lionel Jackson.*

AngelaPickings: *Yes! Go!*

BillyTercer: *You should already be on your way.*

MarjeRoxx: *CharlesChaun, your mother is a fascist.*

Gainesburger: *Go! I'll meet you there.*

It went on and on. Within minutes there were thousands of responses, overwhelmingly positive.

Jackson nodded. "Guess we have our answer."

Bob rushed down the hall to his bedroom. "Let's grab what we'll need and get going before TASE catches on."

Bob's Funbook page fluttered a moment, and then disappeared. Jackson swallowed, rushed down the hall after him.

He found his father with an ancient canvas gym bag, already packed, slung over his shoulder, using his cell to take pictures. He followed Bob's eye to what he was aiming at -- the wedding portrait. "We'll take her with us. Just in case."

"Pop, I think the government already knows. They shut your page down."

"I gotta say I am disappointed they didn't anticipate

our move and block us from doing it at all," he said, shrugging.

Jackson smiled, on his phone again. "Dolores, did we get all of it? Good. Shares? Astounding numbers! Let's get a full press package to every media outlet in existence. Yes, friend or foe! And lead with us getting shut down 'by mysterious parties disrespecting American free speech.' We want to keep it out there. Thanks."

"You slick orchestrator of chaos you," Bob said.

"I had a great teacher."

Bob scooped up Steve. "We'll leave handsome here with Perri and Merle Junior. Steve loves them both so he can stay with—"

The rest of Bob's words were drowned out by gunfire.

Chapter 37

WHEN TASE ARRIVED, JACKSON'S lawyers presented them with injunctions, cease and desist orders, documentation of the premises having been searched by the investigative professionals and a K-9 unit, and so much additional legal paper work Sheriff Merle gave up trying to follow.

The head TASE agent, who identified himself as Spatha, wasn't having any of it. "Step aside."

Sheriff Merle said, "Now, now, boys, we are all gonna play nice in my sandbox, ya'all understand me?"

Spatha turned his stony face and standard opaque sunglasses toward the sheriff for less than ten seconds. "This is no longer your jurisdiction."

"It sure is until you show paperwork to prove otherwise," Sheriff Merle smiled, though his tense body spoke to his actual state of mind.

Spatha seemed bored. "Sheriff, we are taking Robert Murphy and anyone else in that house into custody for Terroristic Activities—"

"That is not what happened," one of the lawyers said too loudly.

Spatha reached over, ripped open the lawyer's shirt, and yanked a wire unit off his body. He tore the mic off the power source and tossed both to the floor. "Are we just arresting this fool for covert acts against the government or do we need to search each of you?"

Another lawyer removed his wire voluntarily. One of Spatha's men ripped it apart and tossed by the first one.

Spatha addressed all of them. "You have now been given an opportunity to cooperate with your government. Anyone else found wearing a wire will be charged with espionage."

Two more gave up their wires. "That's all of them," one said.

Spatha nodded. "Okay, you have avoided prison so far. Next up, let's get all of this out of the way," he waved a hand toward barrage of legal forms. "You can repurpose all of this for your executive lavatory. TASE directives come from POTUS and that supersedes all this noise on the basis of national security. Boom. Done. Next, we are going through that house, confiscating all contraband we find."

The sheriff struggled to maintain his smile. "Mr. Murphy's house was just inspected by trained professionals—"

"Not TASE trained."

While none of them would ever officially admit they were waiting in the wings for the right moment, Jackson's private security team and their K-9 dogs emerged from Bob's house with admirable timing. Almost immediately the dogs began barking and straining against their leashes.

The sheriff gave a nod. Security released the hounds. They charged one TASEr in particular, a tall man with close-cropped red hair. The dogs surrounded him, barking ferociously.

The TASE agents pulled their weapons.

Jackson's private security did the same.

The sheriff's officers raised their shotguns.

"Here we go," Spatha murmured his own weapon instantly in hand.

"Let's all take a breath here, boys," Sheriff Merle called out. "These here dogs are federally-trained to track down illegal substances. Seems to me your man is carrying. Now we all know the True American Security Enforcement Agency does not, and I repeat, does not plant evidence. So you might want to arrest ol'Red over there for impersonating a government agent and interfering with a peaceful, cross-jurisdictional investigation. Have one of your men take him to HQ for processing. Whatcha say 'bout that, Chief?"

Spatha's frozen features tightened slightly. He looked from ol' Red, trapped as he now was in the circle of trained dogs, then to the sheriff and his men, and finally to the private guns-for-hire. "I say I have had enough."

On that coded command, seven bullets sliced through the Sheriff, and when a lawyer took a step foward, ten shots ripped him apart.

The TASE Unit immediately turned their guns on the dogs and Merle's officers. Only one of the sheriff's men got a round off before the slaughter.

That shot went wide.

Private security hit two TASErs before TASE ripped through them, firing dozens of shots per second. Both of the hit TASErs rose, bruised and winded but otherwise unharmed due to high-tech armor under their uniforms.

TASE reloaded and shot any opposition still moving.

Once calm returned and no one except TASE remained, Spatha spoke. "Take the house."

TASE moved forward with purpose, stepping over the corpses without hesitation.

Chapter 38

INSIDE, BOB AND JACKSON hurled looks through the window in time to see Merle shot to death. When TASE started taking out the local cops, both men ran for the kids.

They burst into the kitchen as Perri was heading to the window. Bob scooped her up and tossed her to Merle Jr. "Out the back door!"

Merle Jr. caught his sister in a soft hug, pressing her face to his chest so she wouldn't see anything, and followed them. He snatched up her pink backpack and fell in behind the adults moving across the kitchen.

Bob cradled Steve in his arms, rushed out the back door to where three cars waited, two town cars, and Bob's souped up sedan. The drivers of the town cars stood by their doors, guns drawn. The comedian turned to his son, "These armored?"

"Highest density bulletproof windshield, bulletproof tires, reinforced doors—"

Bob cut him off. "All extra weight that will slow them down." He pointed to the first driver. "You, drive around to the front, draw their attention. Get as far as you can, south on the turnpike if you out run them. If they do run you down, say that you abandoned us and were hurrying back to your family."

He pointed to the second. "You, floor it straight

ahead. Blow through the bushes, turn left on the road just beyond them, get as far as you can. Head north on the turnpike if you get that far. Same alibi once they have you."

Jeremy ran toward the second car. "If they catch us, I can stall them longer. And I'll get media to follow us, giving you more time."

Bob, shocked, called after him. "Jeremy, they aren't playing. Come with us."

"I have to do my job," he said, diving into the second town car.

Jackson started toward the first town car. "I'll delay them in the first—"

"No way." Bob pulled Jackson toward the boring looking four-door. "Fastest car we have," he said, throwing open the door and pushing Merle Jr. and Perri into the back.

"My father," Merle Jr. yelled.

Perri picked up the worry in her brother's tone. "Daddy!"

Jackson tried to reassure her, "Baby, it's going to be all right—"

Bob cut his son off, addressing Merle, Jr., handing Steve to him. "Strap her in, and then Steve. Yourself, too." He twisted the key in the ignition, the engine purred quiet power, and Bob floored it, plunging through the bushes before turning right.

Gunfire sounded as they fled, but it didn't follow them. The agents probably pursued the higher end town cars, assuming the kid took the hotrod, Bob thought, knowing he was rationalizing his ass off.

The kids were losing it. Perri was hysterical, Merle Jr. not much better though he was trying to play it off. Worst sound Bob ever heard, after the rasping of Mary

Angeline's final hours. Nothing else to do but drive on through the baby's tears, through Merle Junior's sobs, through Steve's uncertain moans, through the woods, to the back roads, out of town, across the next county, and onwards, for as long as proved possible.

The kids cried through most of it, Perri eventually exhausting herself and falling asleep, but woke up crying two hours later.

Bob had no idea where he was going but he was in an awful hurry to get there, to get anywhere, in a world that no longer made sense and hadn't for a very long time....

Chapter 39

SPATHA STRODE DOWN THE street shouting orders at the approaching press. "Take cover! This is an active shooter situation! Murphy's team has gone rogue!"

The press hesitated until another volley of gunfire seemed to fly over their heads. Then they retreated. Spatha joined them at the bottom of the street.

"TASE is working to take control of the situation," he reported in a stern commanding voice. "Murphy and an untold number of assailants opened fire from inside the home, targeting local law enforcement first for reasons we have not ascertained at this time."

"But the sheriff is his neighbor...." a reporter challenged weakly.

"At this time TASE is not fully aware of their personal history, so we do not know if there was existing animosity."

"But—" another reporter tried.

Spatha cut him off. "The immediate concern is getting civilians to safety," he insisted. "And while I am aware you all have admirable jobs to do, I am under presidential orders to protect you."

Another series of shots were fired. A National News van's window smashed. The media cringed, throwing themselves to the ground.

"Get into your vehicles and drive to safety. They

have at least one long-range sniper, so go a minimum of five miles. Now!"

With that he disappeared around a van, shouting orders. "Shut those shooters down! We have civilians on scene!"

An adventurous cameraman caught footage of TASE rising to protect them, a wall of gunfire erupting from them, shattering windows, blowing apart Bob's aging aluminum siding.

From somewhere in the house, or so it seemed, bullets ripped the ground close to where reporters were standing.

A reporter squealed, "The sniper!"

The press leapt into vans, stomped gas pedals, and screeched out of the vicinity some already reporting tales of the brave TASE agents facing impossible odds from a celebrity gone mad.

When the last of them was in the distance, Spatha put his left hand onto his tie and all firing ceased. He spoke into a secure communicator. "Have we recovered the vehicles?"

He listened as he walked toward Murphy's house. "Just the driver? Disappointing. How was the chase footage? Good. Make a show of him resisting arrest, and then get him inside our mobile unit. Dose him full of stimulants so he's twitchy and aggressive, and then film the interrogation: three-camera coverage, entirely by the book. We can pad a whole hour with it if POTUS requires multiple episodes."

Spatha listened, nodding, then spoke. "Roger that. Location of the other vehicle? Five minutes out? Fire up all cameras and then chase that dog down. Remember, POTUS wants suspects for the show. No fatalities."

Cutting the communication, he turned to the agents before him. "Alert me immediately if any of our chief suspects are found inside. POTUS wants Murphy and his crew alive for the ratings. Chest cameras back on in three, two, one, go."

The agents moved in. Spatha surveyed the area. There was one private security person trying to stand up. A quick shot and the entire field of engagement was clear. They owned the narrative. Murphy was now a mass-murdering American Terrorist. No one would call out sick from work for this monster. National crisis resolved.

The town car chases would make killer ratings on heavily advertised episodes of *Patriotism Live*. They, of course, would lead to the Murphy episode, which would nab POTUS an Emmy as executive producer and get one for Spatha as director. He would then humbly accept the Medal of Honor from Statler, thanking God, the president, America, his parents, and his loving wife and kids for being his inspiration. Sign the book deal shortly thereafter. Insist on casting approval for the actor to play him in the movie version of his glorious life.

"Damn, it's a good day," he murmured, entering Murphy's home.

Chapter 40

NATIONAL NEWS' TOP-RATED *All-American News With Bling Holsten* was on, the stunning blonde flipping her hair meaningfully as she launched into her "special report" even though every station legal and illegal was covering the same story.

"Tonight the nation is asking itself how their beloved comedic master of mayhem and merriment could morph into a mass murderer. In search of answers, let's look at what we do know."

A series of images played over her shoulder, snapshots of Bob's life, from baby pictures to career and personal highlights.

"Bob Murphy was a comedy superstar, and had been for over 40 years. From his improv days, first as a member of Second City in Chicago and then through his breakout years on SNL, followed by hit movies including *Monster Cops, Princes, Jail Broken*, and *Our Only Boat*, he went from America's Friendly Neighbor to America's Comedy God to America's Cherished Comedy Icon. And now he has betrayed all of us and revealed himself to be a cop-killing clown prince of crime.

"Where did that come from? He had worn his success with grace and ease for years.

"Or so it seemed."

The images shifted to a series of romantic pictures of Bob and Mary Angeline.

"He lived in a large but unassuming house, patronized town stores, went to his grandkids' plays and pageants, supported his town's Little League. His contributions financed half the expenses of that league, and purchased the lighting system — all of it now forever tainted.

"He is a widower who never got involved with another woman after Mary Angeline Murphy nee Calcitrano died, and his devotion to her only endeared him even more to his fans.

"He still wears his wedding ring.

"And this Great American Love Story may be where it all went wrong."

The images stopped on a picture of Mary Angeline on a stretcher, a haggard Bob running beside her.

"There are some reports that Murphy blamed government policy for his wife's death. Perhaps that erroneous rationalization offers some insight into where this comic's life turned tragic."

"In truth, the signs were there long before this week. Since his wife died, Murphy did several odd things that if reviewed from our current perspective, seem to paint an entirely different picture of the Bob Murphy we thought we knew.

"After his wife defied presidential order and flew into an area infested with a highly contagious disease, contracting that fatal illness, Murphy became erratic.

"Rather than drive his numerous cars, he rode an oddly redesigned bicycle, becoming a traffic hazard for town folk."

Paparazzi photos appeared over Bling's shoulder

showing Bob riding his bike, cooking at a grill, and sitting at the counter in Pop's.

"In lieu of the American Dream of fortune and fame, Bob Murphy worked the grill at Little League Opening Days, babysat his grandchildren, patronized small stores in town instead of the nationally accepted mail order houses, and would often show up unannounced at local fundraisers and events. No one protested because he was Bob Murphy, but perhaps that is where we all failed him.

"As a hero-loving culture, we indulged his increasingly bizarre behavior as endearing rather than clear signs of pain.

"And now innocent lives have paid the price while Bob Murphy remains at large, somehow eluding capture.

"And we are all partly to blame for loving him so unconditionally."

A final studio headshot of Bob faded, a waving American flag replacing him.

"But this is an opportunity for the nation to collectively redeem itself. We all know what he looks like, we all can recognize him easily, and so your National News calls for all True Americans to be on the lookout for this fallen icon. Let us help him and secure our own safety by reporting all legitimate Bob Murphy sightings to the number shown below so we can all assist in his immediate capture. Help us get our one-time favorite funny man the help he needs.

"Don't forget to record what you see so we can feature your dedication to our country on *Patriotism Live*.

"We'll be right back after these messages."

In the back seat, beside a sleeping dog and innocent

little girl, Merle Jr. lowered his phone and stared back at the two stunned adults.

The silence lingered even as Jackson started the car, pulled back on the highway and drove further into the black night.

Chapter 41

LIONEL JACKSON WAS NOT accepting of his new reality. The Hattiesburg Freedom Processing Center was populated by displaced Hattiesburg residents and armed "processing coaches" who did very little coaching and a whole lot of intimidating.

Lionel Jackson did not intimidate.

He took a punch well and his return right cross was still surprisingly quick and powerful for an aging actor. Two broken jaws forced the coaches to "advise" Lionel with baseball bats and tasers so they could keep more distance.

Slowed him down a bit.

Didn't break him.

Twenty years of Taekwondo had developed in him powerful defense from both the hand and the foot, resulting in more injured coaches.

As a result, Lionel was thrown into a "meditation encouragement zone" meaning he was caged 24/7 in the camp's yard, exposed to the elements and bathed by high-power hose in front of all the other "applicants."

Still, Lionel kept up a steady stream of taunts and challenges to his captors.

"What am I being charged with, Spineless?"

"C'mon, one of you monkey asses need to charge me with something so I can call a lawyer and sue you homeless!"

Unfortunately, the coaches seemed thrilled to be insulted by a comedy legend. Only one answered back, after Lionel called him Regurgitated Penguin Puss. That star-struck guy insisted Lionel "was not being charged with a crime but merely being processed to make sure you are, in fact, a True American."

"True American this right here, you Nazi wannabe! I was born in Hattiesburg! I'm the truest American you've ever seen, you just don't know what one looks like!"

"They look like us," another said. "Now why don't you just calm down—"

"Charge me or free me, you racist coward! You cannot hold me!"

"You are not being held against your will," another coach said. "You are merely being given time to calm yourself so processing can begin."

"Lipstick on a pig may make it prettier than your Mom, but that doesn't mean I'm gonna date it," Lionel shouted.

One coach walked up close to Lionel's cage, held up an iPad.

Lionel started in immediately. "I don't need you to show me your sister's homemade...."

The scene before Lionel's eyes made his voice trail off. The iPad showed armed, uniformed men storming Bob Murphy's house. The front yard was littered with bleeding bodies.

Lionel slammed himself against his cage, his arm shooting through the bars, trying to grab the tablet.

The startled coach hopped back. Once he recovered, the taunting began. "Your friend is dead. So is your godson. And you were in here where you couldn't help them. What kind of friend and godfather does that make you?"

"Give it here!"

The coach walked away without another word.

Lionel slammed his fists against the bars. "Let me see!"

He slid down, sat in the dirt, hung his head against his knees. Remained in that position until shadows blocked the hot sun roasting his neck. Lionel snorted a deep lungful of air and leapt up, ready to confront the terrorist who had come back to taunt him further.

It wasn't a coach.

Instead, four other prisoners stood before him. Huge. Dark. Built like an NFL defensive line, back when there was an NFL (it withered with the debrowning of America, as did most sports, tech advancements, architectural designs, medical breakthroughs, and so much more). All four were calm. Irritably calm.

"As-salāmu 'alaykum," they said softly.

Lionel wasn't prepared for courtesy. "You need to take that show down the road."

The largest one, easily six-six and built like Atlas, spoke. "Relax, my brother."

"I'm not your brother!"

The next biggest was just six-four; he nodded toward the coaches. "You damn sure ain't their brother."

Lionel looked at the armed white guys and then back to the four mountains before him. After a beat he smirked, voice laced with his signature sarcasm. "Okay, You got me there, *brother*."

They nodded at him on the other side of the bars, but said nothing. So damn calm.

"Look, I'm busy in here. What do you want from me? I forgot my checkbook in my other cage."

"We want nothing from you. Actually, we have something for you."

"Unless it is a set of keys to this place what could you have that would make any kind of difference?"

Another of the four said, "Real news, not the lies they feed you."

The first one leaned close to Lionel's cage. "Your friend and godson are not dead, my brother."

Lionel blinked. "What?"

The second added quietly, "These racists are trying to break your spirit. We heard the actual report. Bob and Jackson Murphy escaped with two unidentified youths—"

Lionel brightened. "The neighbor kids. Gotta be."

"Perhaps. In any event, they are gone. The geniuses in charge gave chase to not one but two decoy cars."

"Good," Lionel said, and then suspicion returned. "Why you telling me this?"

"We would like you to keep up your strength and your faith."

"As much as I appreciate the update, don't take me for a potential member of The Nation, brothers. Me and religion parted ways long ago."

"Underestimating us is the domain of our jailers, brother," the first said. "Islam is our religion, but not the only training we have received."

"Now you got me interested," Lionel said. "What's your training?"

Now the third leaned in close. "Semper Fi."

"Alright, I can work with that."

The first nodded. "Good, because we need you if our

plan is to succeed."

Lionel grinned. "Preach, my brother."

Chapter 42

BO HAD PACED SINCE dawn, sneaking a peek at Amy Brooks' report, snapping it off with a curse, stomping around his quarters, clicking the TV back on, hearing more news about Bob Murphy escaping TASE, pounding the off button again with his thumb, wandering back past his favorite weapon, knowing he shouldn't, fighting his impulse to lash out.

Finally, the leader of the free world couldn't take it anymore. He snatched his presidential phone off the presidential couch, opened the presidential app, and began typing:

> @RealPresidentStatler: Why does filthy rich Murphy even care? He's not a True American. #Don'tBeFooled

Immediately, the responses began:

> Responding to @RealPresidentStatler: @TrueAmericanSam: Elitist, murdering Murphy was never funny. #NotFooled

> @RisingAgain #MurderingMurphy is responsible for every police death on his property. #NotFooled

> @IndieThinker Murphy murdered

no one. Can you say the same, @
RealPresidentStatler? #NotFooledByYou

@TrueAmericanSam to@
IndieThinker you should die, terrorist!
#Don'tBeFooled
@RisingAgain to @IndieThinker, maybe
you need to be reviewed at a Freedom
Processing Center.

@IndieThinker to @TrueAmericanSam,
@RisingAgain Statler fools making
empty threats. You are both cowards
with Twitter muscles. Pathetic.

@ShadowGovernment: Statler rules!

@Get'emAllOut: The choice between
Statler and Murphy is clear; I'll take a
leader over a clown any day.

@IndieThinker to @Get'emAllOut Glad
you chose Murphy, too.

@Get'emAllOut to @IndieThinker I
cannot believe how stupid you are! I
chose Statler!

@IndieThinker But you said you didn't
want a clown....

Statler snarled at the turn in his thread, and kicked
an antique chair he had demanded be moved to the
Wichita White House from the D.C. White House,
shattering the piece of history and putting a dent in a
wall.

"Marlene," the president called out, "Get maintenance up here!"

Chapter 43

MANY MILES NORTH, JACKSON was doing some pacing of his own in a motel room he had rented at three in the morning. He took one at the back of the hotel. It was easier to sneak his father, the boy, the girl, and Steve into the room for the day.

The back roads had been deserted all night, probably in part due to the reported spread of participation in his father's accidental TV appearance. When they did pass the few nighthawks out there they did so at a legal speed in a nondescript car.

What a blessing past impulses can be.

At the height of his fame, Jackson's father found he couldn't go anywhere with his family without being mobbed. It got dangerous when fans started jumping in front of their car. To regain some semblance of normality, he made a big show of driving a flashy Lamborghini while arranging to have a boring sedan fitted with windshields that slightly blurred whomever was inside. That top-secret vehicle was registered to an assistant. That guy received a sizable monthly check just for keeping the paperwork in his name so Bob and family could travel without anyone, even autograph-hungry cops, recognizing them. Jackson had assumed the trick had been abandoned years ago, and was thankful for his father's fidelity to the ruse.

But even the Invisi-Mobile wouldn't protect them enough during the day.

So they hid.

As the much less recognizable face, Jackson got the rooms, always in run down motels where paying a little extra cash "so the wife doesn't see it on the bill" was understood and welcomed.

They slept through the day, Perri and Merle Jr. clocking in the longest hours. Jackson believed they were using sleep to to avoid heartbreaking despondency over their father's horrible death, the poor kids.

Steve slept on the kids' bed, snuggling up next to Perri, or in her open backpack if the room was tense. He was deep in the backpack at the moment.

Jackson and his father slept in shifts, one keeping vigilant near a draped window in case TASE somehow tracked them down.

Jackson's pacing always began during the last hour before dusk, when he grew anxious to get moving across back roads in darkness.

Bob was supposed to be sleeping. Instead, he was doing his best to monitor social media, handing his phone to his son and demanding, "Open something for me," checking that platform, and then demanding Jackson open some other app. This was how he came across Statler's tweet.

"Filthy rich? That phony!" Bob started a reply, deleted it, started two more and deleted those, and then lowered the phone. "I've got too much to say for just 140 characters," he fumed.

Jackson motioned for the phone. It was a burner as they had thrown their more easily traceable personal phones out the car windows almost as soon as they fled

Bob's house. He opened FunBook, hit "go live" and handed it back.

"When you're ready, hit the circle, watch the countdown, and then just talk to everybody for as long as you want. Once you are done, hit the circle again and give it to me. I'll make sure people will find your post pretty quick."

He glanced out the tiny crack between the drapes and then over to his father. "Just keep the camera close so they can't see any backgrounds that might help them ID where we are."

Bob looked at his son for a long beat, nodded with admiration, and then walked into the bathroom. He positioned himself in front of a blank white wall, held up the phone, adjusting it so just his face was onscreen. He hit the button, nodded through the countdown, and then spoke.

"Hey everybody. Didja see President Statler just tweeted that I am somehow fooling you all? And he asked why I cared," Bob said. He took a breath, shaking his head, before continuing. "Why do I care?

"Because the world shouldn't be this messed up;

"Because the powerful and careless shouldn't be able to make our lives worse on a whim;

"Because the influential and greedy shouldn't be able to cut us off from our dreams;

"Because we all should matter more than some political cult of personality;

"And because, damn it, I want the world we were promised. Not the empty assurances of these current dweebs but the guarantees made by the Founding Fathers on sacred documents that still exist.

"Yes, they owned slaves, but even Thomas Jefferson

wrote 'all men are created equal', giving us some hope that we could get there.

"And women's suffrage gave us hope that we could get there.

"And the New Deal gave us more hope.

"And the Civil Rights Movement gave us even more hope.

"What hope are we getting now? How are we advancing our beliefs, this county, the world, our human race?

"The truth is we're not advancing. And we should be. We owe that to ourselves and to each other and to our children and their children and on and on. That is the Idea of America. That any of us, from anywhere in the world, at any level of learning, speaking any language, coming from any economic background, and praying to any god, could come here, and could work hard to make a better life, for us, and for those who come after us.

"That's the Idea of America.

"That doesn't happen anymore because a few want it all for themselves, right now, and forget anyone else, and forget about tomorrow.

"That's not the America I believe in.

"This shouldn't be about a few of us. The Idea of America doesn't work that way. America has to be about all of us, or this is just a shell game, a con, a crime.

"Call it whatever you want, True America, The States, whatever, but if we let the Idea of America die then this is not America.

"And as much as it breaks my heart to say so, right now, we're not America.

"I want us to be the America of promise again. Not

the America that scares its own people, freaks out other countries, imprisons brown people, hunts gay people. I want us to be the America dreamed about in those Founding Father documents, and in those shining moments throughout our history when we created hope for ourselves and for the world.

"Even if it was never completely true, because, honestly, we haven't fully realized the Idea of America, not yet. But we can realize America, together, we can be America, and we should be working toward that, always toward that, because ...the hope of what we might be ... that is the path, the spark, the chance for all of us to finally get to bask in the Idea of America.

"I want to get there. And I want to get there with you. All of you.

"That's why I care, Mr. President. How about you?

"But to get there, to get to the America that was promised in those original documents, to share in that Idea of America in all its glorious political and religious and economic and lifestyle diversity, first we need to get their attention.

"And nothing gets their attention like threatening the money.

"So let's all keep ours, all of us. Let's not spend a penny. We all have enough to last us a few more days. I'm on the run now with just what's in my pockets, so most of you have more than me at the moment, and I'm willing to go hungry for the good of this country.

"Let's do this.

"Let's remind them that there are significantly more of us than there are of them, and if we stop feeding their beast, if we stop buying their stuff, stop supporting their twisted political plans, they fall apart pretty quickly.

"They cannot survive without us, but we can survive by replacing them.

"You see, they have actually taught us some things over these last few years; they've taught us exactly how to survive with almost nothing.

"Turns out that is a weapon we can use.

"Together we can throw the brakes on this whole out of control clown car.

"Until they agree to make some changes. Or get out of our way.

"Until they recognize that we actually matter, let's keep what we have and let them feel forgotten for awhile.

"Let's take our country back, insist on this nation living by the glorious Idea of America by refusing to participate in their limited definition of what True America is.

Why do we care? Because we *are* the Idea of America.

"There's your answer, Mr. President. Thanks for asking."

Bob hit stop, looked to Jackson. "How was that?"

Jackson took the phone, made sure the entire speech went online. When satisfied, he looked up with tears in his eyes, and smiled. "Grand slam homerun, Pop."

Bob shrugged.

Jackson handed the phone back, started packing the few things they had. "Get the kids up, we gotta get out of here."

Bob tossed his few items in his canvas bag. Boom. Done. "What's the rush?"

"After that speech goes viral, they are really going to

want to kill us."

Bob reached over to gently shake Merle Junior. "Now you tell me."

Chapter 44

LIONEL WAS DOING PUSH-UPS in his open-air cage when a coach approached. The actor stood, dusted himself off, and then smiled at the coach, nodding toward the cloudless, sunny sky. "Damn fine morning, ain't it?"

The coach seemed thrown. "Do you think we'll just let you out because you aren't cursing and insulting us?"

Lionel shrugged. "Bob's dead," he said, blessing himself. "You told me that last night, and yes, admittedly, you upset me greatly. But my new brothers, the Muslims you sent over—"

"We didn't—"

"Hey, whatever. I just appreciate you allowing them to talk to me. They made a lot of sense."

"Oh they did, huh?"

"They actually helped you out by asking me point blank how my anger honors Bob's memory. And they're right. He was a positive force to those around him. Since it looks like I am stuck here no matter what I say, I figure let me at least keep the man in my heart by trying to be a more helpful presence in this community, even inside this, ah, meditation center right here."

The coach stared. Finally, he just asked, "Really?"

"Honestly, time will tell, but I'm trying, man,"

Lionel said, shrugging again.

The coach's sarcasm was thick. "And how can we help facilitate these efforts?"

"A bucket of water and some soap would be great — much better than that hose you been drowning me with," Lionel said. He sniffed his shirt, then added, "Maybe some new threads; these are a bit offensive, I'm not gonna lie."

"So you are not asking for release?"

Lionel broke out a broad smile. "Do you realistically think I expect release after my calm and nuanced debate yesterday?"

The coach had to smile. "Point taken," he said. "I'll see what we can do."

With that he walked to the other coaches and they all murmured importantly.

Satisfied with his performance, Lionel hopped up, grabbed the bars above him, and started doing pull ups, crooning a slightly off key version of Al Green's "Let's Stay Together."

Chapter 45

BO WAS LIVID.

Murphy's second live post hit higher numbers than the first. And it increased participation in the national sick out, expanding it to commerce. Ronnie Leland, the Pizza King, called by mid-afternoon complaining that he was down a million orders nationally and threatened to take his losses out of the next campaign donation.

Throughout the day, gas, entertainment, and major retail executives contacted the congressmen whose campaigns they financed, lodging similar gripes. By 6 pm, almost no one was on the street, in the malls, super markets, or even calling into televised shopping shows in most markets across the country. Even online shopping was down dramatically, according to another furious billionaire donor.

"This comedian is costing me money," Bo seethed. "He can't do that, I'm the president!"

He called a meeting of Joint Chiefs of Staff for 7 pm, demanding a plan of action.

"We are at war, gentlemen, make no mistake about that fact," the president always sounded hoarse when he tried to put authority in his voice. "Today that UnAmerican Terrorist, the Murdering Bob Murphy, called for an organized, widespread attack on our economy. We already have major don—

business interests from the energy, entertainment, and retail industries bombarding us with complaints and demands that we take decisive action in the best interests of the nation!"

The various chiefs of staff tried to redirect focus.

"Are you ordering us to deploy military units against native born American citizens?"

"Do you really want the marines to track down a private, American-owned vehicle, sir?"

"Shouldn't that be the purview of the FBI?"

"Or TASE?"

"Or state and local law enforcement?"

Bo slammed his fist on the large oaken conference table, ignoring the pain that shot up to his elbow. "I WANT ALL OF THAT! NATIONWIDE! RIGHT NOW!"

The Secretary of Defense stood, silencing the room. "Commander-in-Chief." He knew Bo loved being called by his military designation.

On cue, the president gave a little involuntary smile.

"Deployment has commenced, sir, but we need to clarify our objective. What is our long-range goal here? Capture? Termination on sight? We must consider the immediate and considerable ramifications that our actions will have on the nation."

Bo sat back in his chair, wanting to issue some baddass order in front of these men, wanting to be a Man of Vision, a Keen Military Strategist, a Tough Guy, wanting to be seen as presidential.

Nothing came to him.

When the silence grew awkward, he stammered, "I'm w-waiting for you to continue your report, general. What do you see as our best option?"

The Secretary of Defense didn't hesitate. "Executing

a very public arrest, and doing so strictly by the book is best," he said. "Show we are not above the law, and neither is he. We will then employ methods of persuasion available to us to secure his renunciation of the entire movement."

The Chief of Staff of the US Army leaned forward, adding, "With his traveling companions as leverage, he will recant quickly, sir."

The Chairman of the Joint Chiefs of Staff waved off the CoSoA. "He's gone too far to recant now. Termination is our best option. Cut the head off the snake."

The Commandant of the US Marine Corps stood up. "And the nation erupts into civil war. Termination is counterproductive to our prime objective: re-establishing the national status quo."

An obviously amused Southern accent rose above the din, interrupting all the official posturing.

"True 'Mericans do have some rights in this country: freedom of speech, freedom of assembly, no matter how dangerous those rights may prove to be."

The speaker was Terry "Shank" Wilkins, Commander-in-Chief of TASE, a new and unwelcome addition to the Joint Chiefs of Staff, there by Bo's insistence. Skank stood and walked to a coffee urn at the side of the room, knowing all eyes would follow him, annoyed by his very presence and incensed that he had the audacity to speak up and then to keep them waiting.

The broad, solid warrior thoroughly enjoyed annoying these pompous relics.

Like most of his "special ops" organization, Shank rose through private military (commonly understood to mean black ops and wet work for hire), surviving bloody skirmishes and outlasting overwhelming odds. He had paid his dues, carried the scars and shrapnel to tell the tale, and disdained the traditions of the older military leaders who looked down their noses at him.

"That Bob Murphy, he surely does have lots of loyal followers," Shank said, pouring hot black coffee into a mug with a presidential seal. "Thang is, he's got just as many rabid enemies. People who believe old Bobby represents everything that is wrong with 'Merica. And these True 'Mericans so love this country they are willing to protect it by any means necessary."

The CoUSMC scoffed, "Your proposed solution is for us to hope some patriot gets to a terrorist even we can't find?"

Shank dropped two cubes of sugar into his black coffee and then smiled at the Joint Chiefs. "Finding him won't be a problem a'tall," he drawled, and then stirred the coffee a bit before he continued. "He's headlining a big rally at the Lincoln Memorial come this Saturday."

The chairman sighed. "Bob Murphy is on the run. He certainly will not be making a public appearance."

"You would think that," the TASE CiC said. He took a sip of coffee, nodded his approval, and then continued. "However, you leaders of men might want to keep a closer eye on where the nation actually lives. Plans are spreading on the Internet. That big demonstration at the Lincoln Memorial is gonna make those old anti-Trump rallies look like a child's birthday party."

The Joint Chiefs flew their fingers across iPads and cell phones. After a few minutes, they collectively glared at Shank.

The chairman said, "There is no demonstration planned, spoken of, or being suggested anywhere on social media."

Shank checked his watch theatrically and then looked up, shrugging. "My mistake. The resistance will come up with this idea in an hour. And when it does, them dedicated rebels are gonna spread the news with the speed and efficiency of Russian hackers."

The Joint Chiefs of Staff stared.

Shank smiled. "Many of our beloved citizenry will assume Ol'Bob himself created the event to finish what he started."

The chairman blurted out, "You—"

"Not me," Shank put a scarred hand to his heart. "Why I been here with ya'all. Could be Bobbie Boy himself. I certainly do not know exactly who would go to all the trouble of organizing a rally on his behalf. That would be crazy."

The Naval commander threw up his hands. "They'll trace the permit paperwork right back—"

Shank cut him off genially. "To Mr. Bob Murphy."

The Marine commander leaned forward. "And if he doesn't show up?"

"Commander, it's a win-win. If 'Merica's former King of Comedy attends, it could be dangerous to his personal health and well being. I mean, who knows who attends these things? But if he doesn't show? And his rally causes many of his followers and many True 'Mericans to die in the obligatory rioting?" Shank shrugged. "Whooooweeee, if Bob Murphy's absence forces your men to swoop in and save the day? Well, in that case, the military will be 'Merican heroes once more, while everybody, on all sides, will blame Bob Murphy for the carnage."

The Joint Chiefs remained unconvinced.

Shank focused on the coffee in his mug. Then he

looked at them from under his dark eyebrows, and spoke out of a sideways smirk. "At least they will after the Internet explodes, condemning him from all sides."

He sat back and offered a knowing eyebrow flick, "Either way, order will be restored to our beloved nation."

He raised his coffee mug in toast. "God bless 'Merica, eh gents?"

Even Bo was speechless.

Chapter 46

MORE THAN A HUNDRED different postings announcing and/or enthusing about Bob Murphy's Free At Last Rally had gone viral within seconds. Nearly a billion repostings, retweets, shares, and commentary threads overwhelmed the Internet, crashing several sites across the country.

People added to the chaos, going live, showing themselves creating banners, dressing as Monster Cops for the event, and leaving for the rally.

Another thing that went viral was a meme from *JailBroken* showing Bob and Lionel breaking people out of jail. The text on it read:

FREE AT LAST!
This Saturday. Lincoln Memorial.
At High Noon We Fire the Goons.

Still another mega viral post featured a clip from *Monster Cops*. The camera panned over the Lincoln Memorial Reflecting Pool, currently reflecting a giant stone Lincoln climbing the Washington Monument a la King Kong, stopping on Bob and Lionel, in full *Monster Cop* gear, prepping to do battle with an advancing pack of rabid congressional werewolves.

LIONEL   How the hell are we gonna stop these fine elected officials?

BOB   With the one thing they all flee from.

LIONEL   Who? They already ate the lobbyists!

BOB   I'm talking about millions of angry registered voters.

(to RAY o.s.) RAY! LIGHTS! CAMERAS! ACTION!

Ray hit lights, illuminating a crowd of Americans advancing to join Bob and Lionel.

LIONEL   Awww, yeah! These puppies don't stand a chance.

This was followed by a black screen. White letters faded in:

This Saturday. Lincoln Memorial.
At High Noon We Fire the Goons.

The saturation across all platforms, apps, and countries was astounding. Russian hackers would be proud.

Chapter 47

BOB MURPHY, WITH NO idea how bad things had just become for all of them, was regretting his last turn. Unwittingly, he drove right toward a hospital; he cursed his stupidity.

At one time, hospitals were calm places of hope and help. These days they were mosh pits of misery, overrun 24 hours a day by those with no insurance and failing health. Thick, heaving crowds shoved each other, trying to get their sick family members closer to shorthanded medical staff they couldn't pay.

The doctors and nurses inside were under siege and took their lives in their hands entering or exiting the building.

Bob saw a nurse being held at gunpoint by a manic guy clutching a wailing infant in his arms. The man screamed, "You are going to take care of my son or you are gonna die tonight!"

Bob's heart sunk, knowing his presence there would only make things worse. How had it all gone so wrong, he thought as he hung a right and headed for the highway.

Chapter 48

MERLE JR. SAW THE overwhelming number of announcements first. He shouted from the back seat, startling Steve, sitting next to him in his specially made travel seat, and Perri, who had been drowsing. "We need to find a motel!"

Bob, who was driving, shook his head. "We can go another hour or two—"

"No we can't," the teen demanded. "Your life and reputation have been hacked."

Jackson turned to the kid. Merle Jr. held up his phone to the lawyer.

Jackson took the device, read, then scrolled, read more frantically, paling as he did. Finally, he said, "He's right; we need to find a motel. Now!"

Chapter 49

HIGHWAY HEAVEN –HOURLY RATES Available was the next motel to sleaze its way into view. Reluctantly, Bob pulled in. Jackson jumped out to register. His father drove around back.

Once inside Room D13, Merle Jr. set up the listless and teary-eyed Perri with the last supplies from her backpack: a juice box, a snack sized container of HoneyNut Cherrios, her coloring book, and a 24-box of Crayolas.

Merle Jr. turned on the TV.

"No news. It just hurts my heart," Perri complained.

By her side, Steve agreed. "Yip."

Merle Jr. gave her the remote. "Whatever you want, Periwinkle."

The nickname failed to brightened to tiny beauty.

Saddened, he crossed the small room to where Jackson opened a laptop, signed onto one of the dozen dummy identities Dolores had created for them. The guys scrolled through the overwhelming ocean of announcements claiming that Bob Murphy, organizer of the Free At Last! Rally on Saturday at the Lincoln Memorial, "wants everybody to join him." Some included a smirking picture of Bob with a cartoon dialogue balloon that read, "Doctors notes available for those 'out sick'!"

Bob asked Jackson, "Did your people do this?"

Jackson said no, and looked at the teen.

"Don't look at me," Merle Jr. protested, "I'm the one who told you guys."

Perri called over from the bed where she was coloring and watching a cartoon. "Don't look at me, either, I'm not even allowed on the iPad yet," she said.

"Someday, darling," Merle Jr. assured her.

"Daddy says I can on my next—" she began, and then burst out crying.

Steve scurried over to her. She hugged him, sobbing. Suddenly her sobs gave way to a shocked scream as if she'd been slapped.

The three guys jumped, their eyes following Perri's pointing finger to the TV.

Patriotism Live had interrupted her cartoon about singing bears.

Bob immediately recognized why the little one had screamed.

Merle Jr. took Perri and Steve into his arms, hugging both gently to his chest and carrying them away from the television. She cried and pressed her face into his shirt.

On a split screen, *Patriotism Live* showed both Pop and his son being captured.

On the left, Pop was being dragged out of his burning store, arms tied behind him, legs bound at the knees and ankles. The left side of his face was swollen, his nose broken and bleeding.

His captors, heavily inked Nazis with bad haircuts and swastika T-shirts, whooped and celebrated as they hung him by his roped arms from the lift of a tow truck. Behind them, others carried a half-closed body bag. An arm dangled from it, wearing the bracelets and wedding band Bob knew belonged to Pop's wife.

"Eleonore."

Incredibly, the right side of the screen was worse, showing a dynamic chase as bikers with SS lightning bolts on their helmets raced by whomever was filming them dragging a large fishing net between their hogs.

Inside the net was a struggling human being.

Someone screamed, "We captured us a fag!"

The amateur videographer was riding on the back of another motorcycle. He managed to capture the net being released, the captive rolling to a scrapped and bloody stop, followed by the sounds of breaking bones and screams of agony as the camera's ride ran over the man in the net.

The video feed cut to another angle, a clear shot of the apprehended.

It was Pop's son, Terence, writhing in agony, his screams panicked and excruciating.

A torso wearing a confederate flag T-shirt came into view carrying a shotgun. "Shuddup," that person ordered before slamming the butt of the weapon down and out of view.

There was a sickening thump.

Terence made no sound after that.

The confederate spoke again. "All that cryin's bad for ratings."

Off camera, a crowd bellowed with rough laughter.

Jackson snapped off the TV.

It took nearly a half hour for Merle Jr. to soothe Perri to sleep. When she was finally out, the guys sat as far from her as possible and whispered together.

Jackson nodded back to the TV, "Those are the

same sort of guys hunting us."

"Them and the military," Bob added.

Merle Jr. leaned forward, meeting their eyes with unwavering determination. "We can't keep Perri in this situation. It is neither safe nor healthy. What are our options?"

"Run," Jackson said, "or run faster."

Bob shook his head. "Not that simple," he said. "The interrupting of a cartoon network suggests they probably broke into programming on all stations to show that capture. That was done to send us a message. They are going after our people."

Merle Junior's frown deepened. "They went after our people at your home, or have you forgotten our father so soon?"

"Not for a second," Bob assured the teen.

"Of course not," Jackson added.

Bob asked his son, "Are you sure your kids are safe?"

"Bo has zero jurisdiction in Cali," Jackson said.

"Can you send Perri to be with them?"

"It can be arranged."

"Then arrange it, please," Merle Jr. pushed.

Jackson stepped away to make a call.

Merle Jr. switched topics. "Meanwhile, the president or someone supporting him has launched a hack attack guaranteed to defeat your online plea. If you don't attend this rally, people will think you abandoned them. The president and the media will make sure of that by painting you as a coward betraying millions of loyal followers. But should you embrace the insanity of showing up, there is a one hundred percent chance of violence against you."

Bob nodded to the kid. "It's good to have a choice."

"Wit won't save you against these bullies," Merle Jr. warned. "They are aiming at every vulnerability you have."

"He can just say no," Jackson insisted, rejoining them. "The public knows Statler's storm troopers are after him. They'll understand he'd be in danger."

Merle Jr. leaned over the laptop, typed a few words, sat back. "As I said, one hundred percent."

Onscreen was a "news item" written and published by Statler's own people. Beside a picture of Statler in his best presidential pose was a quote:

"Murdering Bob Murphy should know I am granting him his right to free speech for this rally of his, but I expect a peaceful, voluntary surrender to proper authorities immediately afterwards. We must allow the legal process to take its course. If he did nothing wrong, if he is a True American, he has nothing to fear. God bless True America."

Jackson sighed. "Checkmate."

"Nope," Bob shook his head. "I gotta believe we still have a few moves left." He stood up but did not start cleaning. "I'm going to be honest with you, I loved Mary Angeline, built my life around her. She was the reason I was able to achieve everything that I accomplished. She was my inspiration, and she pushed me to go farther than I thought possible. And I'm starting to think she might be angry with me over how I have lived my life since she passed."

Bob saw their looks. "I know Mary Angeline is gone. I miss her every day. That's where I made my mistake; I stayed in a loop of our places, trying to keep those last memories going as if they were all I had left. I feared living my life. That's where a lot of us fail; we get wrapped up in our own concerns, our own hurt, and we forget that we are part of a larger community.

"And too many of us have been so wrapped up in our own dramas, we left too much to others. Before we knew it, our distractions left them free to drive us into the ground. That's no excuse. We're complicit; we let it happen.

"But we're waking up now, and maybe we need to thank our crappy leaders for shaking us out of complacent slumber.

"Maybe that's how we turn this nightmare around. People are reacting, they want an enormous event like this—"

Jackson cut him off. "Which could get you killed."

Bob shot back, "And a life on the run won't?"

"It will buy time so our lawyers can make a case to resolve this insanity."

Bob laughed. "Which insanity? Everything has gone too far."

"And it's your responsibility to fix it all?"

"Not mine alone," Bob insisted, pointing to the laptop. "Look at that traffic! Clearly people need to participate."

"We can't take the kids," Jackson insisted.

They both looked at Merle Jr.

He frowned deeply. "I'm no kid, but even I agree; we need to get Perri out of this, even if I have to go with her."

Bob nodded. "You are the only one I trust to make sure she gets to safety, Merle."

"Junior," the kid corrected.

"When you act like a man you should be addressed as a man," Bob said. "I am not forgetting your father, I'm honoring the man you've become. He would be proud to see Perri is in good hands. You'll protect her, Merle."

Merle inhaled deeply, let it out, nodded his thanks. And then all three men looked at Perri asleep on the bed, her little hand still clutching a soft blue crayon.

"I will," her brother said.

Chapter 50

CONGRESSMAN GARLAND "BABE" EARLY took his girth onto National News to point out to an outraged Bling Holsten that TASE's inability to track down the car that Bob Murphy is using has led authorities to believe that this so-called comedian has kept either an unregistered vehicle or an illegally registered vehicle for many years.

"What does that reveal about the real Bob Murphy," Bling soft pitched him.

"Well, Bling darling, this reveals a possible conspiracy to mislead the people's understanding of who Bob Murphy really is. He and his miscreants are flaunting their wealth and power in the faces of regular True Americans who need to obey the law. We, as a nation, put our faith in Murphy as a God-fearing, taxpaying citizen but it seems that there was much more going on behind the scenes with this liberal manipulator of minds than we were originally led to believe. We as a nation must re-evaluate who this man is 'cause it seems very clear to me that he had malfeasance on his mind for quite some time. We may even be able to re-interpret his films as actually sending out subliminal anti-American messages to an unsuspecting public."

Bling patted his arm. "This is what we get for

trusting the Hollywood elite."

The Congressman shook his head sadly, sending his jowls wagging. "It's a pity to think we have been bamboozled for all these years by a public figure posing as our funny cousin while all the time he was planning the demise of this Great Nation. But I have faith that, together, we can weather this storm."

Bling broke into a dazzling TV smile. "Yes we can."

Chapter 51

THE RELUCTANT RESIDENTS OF the True American Processing Center of Hattiesburg, Missouri, started gathering around Lionel's cage around 7 pm. The guards didn't think anything of the first six or so, but when the numbers hit double digits, they started to shoo them away.

"Hey, Captain," Lionel called out, "don't blame them; this is my fault."

Lionel's primary coach walked over to him. "I thought you were turning over a new leaf."

"I can't tell you about any leaves, Coach, but I am trying to help here."

"By gathering an unruly crowd?"

"Nobody's unruly here," Lionel said, biting down on his temper. "I told them if they came around I'd put on a show. Tell stories, some jokes. Lighten the mood for an evening. It'll damn sure make your job easier. You got a problem with that?"

The coach studied him as if searching for weapons or something.

Lionel leaned into it, pulling his pockets inside out, and then lifting his new shirt. "Nothing. See? Want me to drop my pants too? I can, but we'll need a bigger cage...."

The coach laughed. "You still got it, brother," he

said like they were old friends.

Brothers don't imprison each other, you mother—
Lionel swallowed his thought, nodded instead, and quickly stepped toward the gathering crowd. "Grab a piece of dirt, y'all. Kids in front," he called. "Wanna know how we got your favorite heroes to defeat the aliens?"

The kids cheered and Lionel was off, spinning yarns from his more recent superhero movies to their utter delight, peppering the tales with double entendre jokes the kids giggled at for one reason and the parents enjoyed on a whole other level. He kept it up for an hour, the crowd growing steadily until all the coaches were around the perimeter, supposedly keeping order but actually laughing along with their captives.

After about 90 minutes, Lionel announced that it was time for the bigger kids to get the smaller ones to bed because the next set of stories were "not for little innocent ears." Once the kids and adolescents were off to the crappy family bunkers, Lionel, with quick glances to make sure the coaches were locked in to his performance, got downright bawdy, doing cherished bits from his stand up career including "Trouser Snakes Return to Belfast," "Little Bit of Better Batter," and not one but two stories from his legendary stand-up character Two-Hand Jimmy. In that beloved hobo persona, Lionel performed "There Came a Stankfoot" and the infamous "Spellcasting Hos of Alabama," which inspired wave after wave of howling laughter — especially from the coaches, Lionel observed — until its chaotic finale was met with a standing ovation.

Lionel took deep bows first to the left — as he confirmed those coaches were still there — and then to the right — confirming coaches were applauding on that side, too, and then to the center, where he saw the remaining coaches were clapping and whistling completely unaware of the dozen men standing a short distance behind them in full riot gear.

That had been the plan — Lionel was to give a performance the coaches just couldn't miss while the marines broke into the weapons storehouse and suited up in armor and weaponry. As he took his final bows, Lionel enjoyed deep satisfaction in knowing his comedy allowed the warriors to put their liberation plan into motion.

Now Lionel just had to avoid getting shot when all hell broke loose.

The dozen Muslim marines spread out as Lionel milked the applause, pretending to have a heart attack – another famous routine—keeping everyone riveted on him until the dozen military veterans got into position. When Lionel raised his fist as the agreed upon signal, they each fired point blank into a coach's brain.

The coup was executed with precision. Weapons and keys were taken from the corpses, and one marine freed Lionel.

The crowd was unsure how to react. Many were convinced troops would appear from the shadows to kill them all. When that didn't happen, someone in the crowd asked, "What do we do now?"

Lionel answered, "I say we wake the kids and go home!"

Chapter 52

AFTER MUCH DISCUSSION, BOB, Jackson, and Merle decided to fight fire with fire and Bob went live again.

He stood in front of a motel wall, a generic print of a forest scene partially covering a large, diagonal crack.

"Hey," he began, "I thought I'd pop on and tell you two things: all those rally announcements you've been seeing didn't come from me — how could I do all that work while on the run from people who murdered all the officers at my house and then blamed me? And the other thing is, if they really want us to rally that bad, let's do it, but we'll do it our way.

"We will not riot or fight or do violence. That might be them; that isn't us.

"If we go to Washington, D.C., let's go there as the Founding Fathers intended, to discuss ideas, and vote for change.

"Right now there are people in power many of us don't agree with. We can't expect them to read our minds. It is on us to express ourselves, to exercise the rights and freedoms this country was built upon. Because the truth is, the Founding Fathers were wild men geniuses who knew the best thing for us would be to debate everything until we reached consensus.

"That's how we get to 'a more perfect union.'

"But expressing what we think in a pithy meme is not enough. Writing an angry Facebook post or a snarky Tweet is not enough. Entrenching ourselves, isolating ourselves, communicating only with those who agree with us is not the way to perfect this union.

"You know what? I'm not sure I really knew any of that when Winston Miller FaceTimed me. I just saw it as him tricking me into going public. But sometimes we need to be pushed forward, you know? I understand that now, so thanks, Winston Miller. You may have ruined my peaceful zombie existence but you woke me up to life.

"So here's what I'm proposing: let's go ahead with a peaceful rally, but first, let's figure out together what we want to communicate to our leaders, how we want to move our country forward. In the comment section below this thing, I'm asking that you write three positive sentences about what we want this country to accomplish, what we want this president and this congress to do for us and with us.

"Let's not make it negative or rude. You know who you are, ya wacky trolls.

"Let's seriously consider what we want for this country and then we'll read out the results at the rally in a peaceful, productive way that everyone will understand.

"God bless the America we love and miss."

Jackson confirmed it went out live. The three men exchanged nervous looks.

A very theatrical cough turned their attention to Perri who was petting Steve on her lap as she met their gaze with an approving nod. "Good job, guys."

It broke the tension and everybody laughed.

Within moments, entire swathes of the country showed they agreed with Perri.

"We did it," Bob enthused. "That was so positive and pro-peace that Bo will be hard pressed to keep tagging me as a terrorist."

Jackson and Merle just frowned at him.

Bob tried again. "Guys, we're at the heroic banding together montage now; we're golden!"

And then came thunderous pounding on the door.

Chapter 53

"OPEN UP, IT'S THE POLICE!"

This was followed by a muffled giggle and then, at a lower volume, "I told him it was the police, man!"

Another, more nasal voice disapproved. "Don't tell him it's the police, dude! You'll create a bad first impression!"

Mortified by that possibility, the first voice adopted a much more earnest tone. "Bob Murphy! It's not the cops! It's just us, man! Open up, Bob Murphy!"

Bob motioned for Perri to put her head down and pretend to sleep.

Perri gave him a thumbs up and dove onto the pillow.

Bob opened the hotel room door just wide enough for Perri to be seen. Jackson stood behind it with a chair raised bizarrely over his head.

Bob smiled, putting a finger to his lips. "Guys, sshh, my niece is taking a nap."

Two potheads right out of central casting stood outside the door. They peered in, saw the "sleeping" Perri and made comically sincere "Oh!" faces, going up on their tiptoes for no reason at all.

The guy with the nasal voice whispered, "Oh, dude, we're so sorry! We'll be really quiet. We just wanted to say hello to, like, The Bob Murphy."

The first guy gushed, "You are The Man, man!"

Bob nodded greetings. "Thanks, fellas. How did you know where I was, guys?"

Nasal whispered with ridiculous enthusiasm. "Oh, dude! We saw you go live!"

Bob chuckled, asked again. "I still have to ask, how did you know where I was?"

The apparent brains of the duo gasped, and then said. "Oh! Because of that crack in the wall behind you when you was live, man. I made that crack in that wall with my head last time we had a party here, dude!"

Bob nodded his head some more. "You partied in this very room? I thought it had a good time vibe to it."

"You know that, Bob Murphy!" They both nodded back at him for a while and then Brains asked, "Why are you here in town, Bob Murphy?"

Nasal added, "Are you, like, making a film around here, Bob Murphy?"

Bob raised an index finger to his lips, and then patted his hands out in front of him in a "let's keep this quiet" gesture that often preceded the sharing of a really big secret. "I'm not supposed to say, fellas, but we are thinking about filming here in a couple of months. We are trying to scout locations. Do you know your way around here, guys?"

"Oh yeahhhhhhh, man! We know this place like the back of, like, the back of, we really know this place, man," Brains bragged. Then a light of dim wattage went off in his eyes. "Hey! Are you making, like, our kind of movie, man?"

Bob nodded seriously. "As a matter of fact we are," he said, "But only if we can find the right locations, if you know what I mean." Bob said with a knowing wink.

"We can definitely help you with that, Bob Murphy!

We know all the locations around here!"

"If you can find us ten we can pay you $1,000 for each location."

Brain looked like Bob had shown him God. "You're shitting us."

"I would not shit gentlemen of your caliber."

"Dead ass?"

"Completely," Bob agreed. "Can you guys find those locations?"

Nasal sort of bowed, speaking in a solemn voice, "We most definitely will, Bob Murphy."

Brain nodded sagely. "Mos def."

"Then we'll meet you here tomorrow, say around 9 a.m.?"

The two burnouts looked pained.

Bob suppressed a chuckle. "If you don't mind, can we make it noon-ish?"

The dudes nodded their heads vigorously.

"We can definitely do noon for you, man," Brain assured.

Nasal crossed his heart, and promised, "We will be here with ten locations for the serious dinero at noon manana, Bob Murphy!"

Bob gave his best smile, "All right, guys, you really saved us here! Thanks. We will see you then."

He closed the door and listened. They could hear the pair high-fiving and congratulating themselves.

"Dude! We're in show business!"

"We are making a movie with Bob Murphy!"

Peaking through the narrow crack in the drapes, Bob watched the two dudes meander across the parking lot celebrating the score of their lives.

Once they rounded the corner, he turned to the

others. "Perri, performance of a lifetime! Everybody, pack up right now. We gotta get out of town immediately."

Chapter 54

JACKSON PAID FOR ANOTHER night in an attempt to throw off any suspicious locals and then they loaded up the car and took off. Putting distance between themselves and the motel wasn't good enough; they also had to face cold hard facts.

In the front passenger seat, Jackson glanced back at Perri playing with Steve. She raised his tiny paws and shook it at Bob's son. "Steve, do you think it is time we go home," she asked. Steve nodded. "Thank you, Steve." She met Jackson's amused glance with one of surprising steel. "Home, please. Now."

Merle, buried in his phone searching for updates on their dilemma, met Jackson's eyes briefly. "As always, she's in charge," he said. "Answer your queen."

"We'll get you there, your highness," Jackson bowed to Perri, who giggled, that sound a shaft of golden sunshine in this endless night.

He turned in his seat to face forward again, whispering so only Bob heard. "Dolores is having bodyguards meet us somewhere and will fly with them to California personally. They'll be safe."

Perri said, "We don't have port passes."

"Passports, Periwinkle," Merle corrected.

Jackson turned back to the child, twisting himself until he could aim his phone straight on at Perri. "Give me a serious face, honeybunny," he said

She did.

Jackson took ten photos on his camera, making adjustments as he progressed. Then he did the same for Merle.

Bob, who was driving, glanced at his son snapping away. "Don't tell me; Dolores's going to work some magic and turn these poorly lit car pics into acceptable passport photos?"

"She'll start the magic," Jackson replied, sitting properly in his seat once more, sending the best selections to his outrageously resourceful executive assistant. "The firm sending the bodyguards will take care of the rest."

Merle leaned forward in his seat. "The rest?"

"Bodyguards, transport to a private plane, transport to California."

"You're gonna have us live with strangers? In California?"

Perri patted her brother's arm. "Merle, it's okay," she assured, "Dolores is magic and I would like to see where Uncle Bob used to work."

Merle gazed at his little sister for a long beat, and then squeezed her hand. "If it's good enough for you, Periwinkle, it is good enough for me."

Bob pushed the gas down a bit more. With safety suddenly a possibility for any of them, his grip on the wheel tightened, knuckles whitening as if he feared even this thin hope would be stolen from them too....

Chapter 55

BACK AT THE HOTEL, Nasal rolled fat joints as Brain bragged on the phone. "Mannnn, I'm tellin' you, we are working for Bob Murphy now," he insisted. "We're definitely good for the money."

He listened, a look of disappointment crossing his face. "Are too, man! And look, look, look, you front us and we'll introduce you to THE Bob Murphy. How'bout that, man? Yeah, I definitely know where he is! *Highway Heaven* Motel, D-13, my dude!"

Elation lit his face. "Cool! Yeah, we'll wait right here, D-22. Come over soon, they're doing Tom Petty on *Rock Legends*. Yeahahahahahhaaha!"

Chapter 56

WHILE THE RESIDENTS OF Hattiesburg gathered their kids and meager possessions, the marines loaded up trucks with all the supplies they could find. Food storage units were emptied, the contents put on camp trucks. Cases and cases of bottled water were loaded. And the entire munitions supply facility was placed carefully in a separate vehicle the marines supervised themselves. They put the elders and youngest in transport vehicles, but everyone else had to walk. It was slow going but spirits were high.

Freedom and the promise of home inspired the long traumatized citizens to dream again. Lionel was moved by the beautiful universality of their aspirations.

"All I want is to sleep in my own bed," one said.

"I want to stand under my shower for three days."

A guy chuckled. "Not to be rude, but there's another use for that room," he said. "Some privacy and store bought TP? That would prove this nightmare is really over."

"I want to cook a meal on my stove, with my pots and my pans, and set it on our table, using our plates and knives and forks and spoons. And I want Tookie to use his favorite plastic *Stars Wars* cup, and real napkins. "

"I'm coming over to your house," another giggled.

An older gentleman limped as he walked, having given his seat in the transport vehicle to a young mother and her baby. A gallant gesture but now his leg was getting worse. A woman near him took his elbow. "You want us to get you a seat in one of the trucks?"

The older man smiled. "That's kind, Shallah, but the next seat I want to use is in my living room, with a cup of coffee and one of my Walter Mosley novels."

Lionel Jackson overheard most of these exchanges as he made his way to the marines. "These people are all talking about domestic bliss," he told the largest one.

"Good to know what one is fighting for," the marine answered.

"So you think they know they're going to have to fight to keep what's theirs?"

The marine kept marching, head on a swivel. "When have we ever not had to fight for what's ours?"

Lionel nodded. "I hear that, but they're thinking 'Great God Almighty, I'm free at last.'"

"We'll make the situation clear once they see their houses again. After they touch their property. Smell home. Memory keeps them walking now: reality will put fire in their hearts. That's when we'll explain what's coming."

"Get me a working phone and I'll pay for the lawyers we'll need. Get my godson on the case," Lionel offered.

"Much appreciated. That's the long-term war," the soldier agreed. "Right now we got to get them onboard for the more immediate battle."

Lionel felt a small spark of hope. "So you have a plan?"

"Marines always have a plan."

"Semper Fidelis indeed," the comedy icon nodded, marching a little taller now toward home.

Chapter 57

MERLE FOUND THE LATEST Amy Brooks report on YouTube. Curious as to why it was only a few minutes long he plugged in ear buds and hit play.

The first thing he noticed was that once again she wasn't in a studio. Actually, she didn't even have a set behind her. Amy Brooks was standing in front of a brick wall, clearly recording on a phone held by a shaky hand. The white streak in her hair seemed wider, and she needed a brush and some make-up. And better lighting. And a proper microphone. Maybe a camera operator other than herself, one with a steadier hand.

"This is Amy Brooks. We may not be able to broadcast regularly for awhile," she said, eyes wide, lips chapped, breathing elevated. "Those who would shut us down are … pursuing aggressively."

A voice off camera shouted, "They're here! Go! Go! Go!"

Amy ran, the screen view flailing as her thumb crossed over it and the broadcast was cut….

Merle shut down his phone, plugged it into the charger, and then stared out the window. Amy posted it so she must have escaped, he reasoned, but dark forces were closing in one many fronts. How long until they closed around those in this vehicle, he thought, his gaze turning to Perri sleeping next to him, "We gotta get out of here," he murmured.

"What's that," Bob asked.

"Just drive faster, please," Merle pleaded.

Chapter 58

"HE'S HERE!"

Brain went to the window sure the headlights shining through the dirty drapes belonged to Johnny Crispino's weed mobile.

Nope.

"Dude! They're filming a scene across the way!"

Brain marveled as huge Klieg lights lit up the night and actors performing as black-clad soldiers crowded around D-13. With a boom they knocked down the door and ran inside—

A matching boom shattered D-22's door. More black uniforms rushed in.

Brain backed against a wall as black uniforms swarmed the two of them aiming huge guns point blank.

They weren't actors, man, Brain realized.

Nasal raised a thick blunt to the soldiers. "Wanna light up?"

The light he received was a muzzle flash.

Chapter 59

BOB DROVE IN SILENCE for a while before Jackson spoke. "How did you know?"

Bob tossed him a questioning look.

"The dudes, how did you know they were dangerous?"

Bob chuckled mirthlessly. "I've met a lot of fans. Every once in awhile one stands apart. Those two didn't mean harm but they weren't going to be satisfied with an autograph or a picture, and they were definitely going to tell everyone they knew where they met us until we were overrun or the wrong person heard."

"What does a 'wrong person' want?"

"Blood."

Jackson stared at his father hoping for a punch line. Bob glanced back, the fire in his eyes confirming none would be forthcoming.

They both looked forward, through the dirty windshield at the empty road unfolding before them, endless, brutal, and dark.

Chapter 60

IT SEEMED POETIC THAT the residents reached Hattiesburg just as the sun ascended over the rise. They climbed toward the new day excited, energized, and so ready for the promise of home.

That promise plunged as the first of them reached the crest and Hattiesburg came into view.

A small jolt through the marine's body gave it away. The horror grew as the Hattiesburg residents joined him. Each held in their hearts a highly personal image of what they would see, but the devastation was universal.

Every house, sidewalk, street corner, and blade of grass had been demolished.

Hattiesburg was gone.

Their entire hometown had been completely, utterly bulldozed out of existence.

In Hattiesburg's place was an immense construction site with materials and trucks and plows and new buildings — high end McMansions were being erected where their life once was.

A large, ornate sign proudly announced the construction of The Corinth Estates.

The old man with the limp asked, "How could they knock down our houses?"

A mother whispered, "Where did they put my kids'

clothes?"

Another cried, "What did they do with out photo albums?"

A marine growled, "Our paperwork, mortgages, academic degrees, military honors, financial records—"

Lionel spat out the end of that thought. "Our lives."

Behind the new construction of The Corinth Estates was a crater gray with ashes and blackened with burned detritus. It was half filled in with new dirt.

Lionel could hardly breathe. "Here it is, folks: True America."

Chapter 61

DOLORES'S ARRANGEMENTS TOOK BOB, Jackson, Merle, and Perri to a huge abandoned mall. Directions were to drive to the loading docks around back at 3 a.m.

They arrived at 3:15 to no signs of life. Not even a stray dog or scrounging rat. The place was a cratered moon of broken blacktop and hollowed entranceways.

Despite the lack of life around the mall, inside their car, the air was crackling with tension.

"This is not a good place, Uncle Bob," Perri quivered.

"I can't shake the feeling," Merle insisted, "that we are being watched."

Bob turned to Jackson, "You sure about this place?"

"If we want to go along with the plan we've got to get to the back of this mall."

"Then at least kill the lights," Merle suggested.

"And hurry," Perri whispered.

Bob did both, and the car accelerated into the darkness. He did his best to miss the potholes, but caught one with a loud crunch as they passed a main entrance.

Almost immediately a roar went up from inside the ruined mall and a single headlight snapped on like the opening of Cyclops' ominous eye.

Merle leaned forward, at the same time thrusting a protective arm in front of his little sister. "Biker?"

Bob glanced at his side view mirror and floored it. "Wish it was only one."

Merle and Jackson stared through the sedan's rear window dumbfounded as a biker gang roared out of the mall.

Perri put her arms around Steve, her lower lip quivering. "Don't be scared, Steve," she whimpered.

Steve nuzzled her face, licked a tear off her cheek as the sound of roaring engines grew closer.

Chapter 62

LIONEL AND THE MARINES got the townspeople to the construction site. The citizens wandered aimlessly, approximating where their homes had been. A few collapsed on the sites of their former properties, overwhelmed. Others began to attack the new structures, kicking at support beams.

The marines put a stop to that.

"We are going to need these buildings to live in," the largest one explained.

Lionel joined in. "They stole our town from us? We're stealing it back."

Some cheered.

The big marine raised a hand, silencing everyone. He cocked his head to the side and listened. So did everyone else.

Together they heard a rumbling in the distance.

Lionel saw the first truck roar over the rise, a Confederate flag flying in the headlights of those coming up behind it.

The trucks kept coming, red necks and backwoods militia men hanging off the sides, screaming like Comanche (the irony was surely lost on them) and waving shotguns and rifles as they descended upon the former residents of Hattiesburg.

Chapter 63

THE BIKERS CHASED THE sedan, closing in on each side. Suddenly a thick chain swung through the darkness, a sharp hook at its end digging into the door next to Perri. The rider who launched it roared off.

The chain went taut; the sedan was yanked to one side until Perri's door was torn away.

Bob spun out wildly before regaining control of the car.

Another biker raced up to the new opening, reaching for Perri. Merle covered her with one arm and thrust his other hand into the biker's face, firing a taser he held right into the jerk's surprised eyes. The predator screamed and fell off his hog in spasms. His Harley tumbled end over end into another rider.

"Thank you for saving me, Merle," Perri whispered and kissed her brother on the cheek.

"Always, Periwinkle."

The sedan slid a bit as Bob took the last corner and then there they were, not one but two gleaming helicopters.

Jackson shouted, "Go! Go! Go!"

Merle eased the backpack open and released Steve's safety strap. He slipped the dog into the bag and zipped it almost completely closed. When Perri looked at him concerned, Merle leaned in close so she could hear him, "To keep him safely with us, hon."

Perri nodded, tears welling up in her frightened eyes.

Bob skidded to a stop as close to the 'copters as he dared.

Jackson leapt out and ran for the waiting pilots and the armed bodyguards. "Shoot those bikers," he commanded.

Four bodyguards raised their Glocks and fired with impressive precision, dispensing the nearest riders with ease.

The rest of the bikers were maybe 200 yards away, racing forward, pulling weapons of their own.

Bob jumped out and slid over the hood to where Merle and Perri were climbing out. He pulled them to him in a desperate hug. "These guys will protect you both and get you to Dolores! She'll make sure you are safe! We'll get to you as soon as we can, I promise!"

Merle was uncharacteristically shook. "I never got you that Second City bootleg! I'm so sorry—"

He hugged them both closer. "None of that matters now. And I'm the one who's sorry! I'm so sorry for all of this! There's no time for—"

He glanced over his shoulder. The remaining bikers were 100 yards away and rushing relentlessly toward them. He embraced them urgently. "Just know I love you!"

Bob scooped up Perri and ran to Jackson at the helicopters. Merle followed.

"Which of these men do you know the longest," Bob demanded of his son.

Jackson pointed to one pilot. "Fifteen years," he shouted. Then he waved over two of the bodyguards. "Thirteen years."

Bob handed Perri to one of them. "With your lives," he demanded.

"Roger that," he said.

"We'll get them home safe, sir," the other promised, and they placed the girl in the copter beside her brother. Merle strapped Perri in as the gunmen placed their bodies between the kids and the armed bikers, taking four more out. One of them grabbed a headset, shouted a command, and slammed the 'copter door. The pilot rose and arced away quickly.

Merle held Perri to his chest as they flew off.

Tears in his eyes, Bob followed Jackson into the other helicopter, their bodyguards still firing, blowing out tires and ripping through legs of any riders in sight. The rest screeched to stops to avoid running over their brothers. One of bodyguards tossed them a farewell grenade.

As they rose and flew out of the bikers' range, the bodyguard motioned for the Murphys to don headphones.

"Your kids will be in Canadian airspace within minutes," the pilot assured. "They will remain in that air space and then fly over Pacific international waters before circling back to Cali. They will never be in the States' airspace so will be safe from the American military planes." He paused a second, and then said, "We can follow them or fly to DC. The latter is significantly more dangerous. Your call."

Jackson nodded toward the kids' copter already diminishing into the distance, casting his vote.

And in a moment that shamed him, Bob faltered. He wanted to follow, to run, to escape, to just make this entire nightmare stop. Let everyone fend for themselves, that's the way of America nowadays, isn't it? If they got to California there would be no extradition, no more risk. His assets were protected through Jackson's Los Angeles offices; they would all be wealthy, privileged, safe. Merle and Perri could go to the finest schools, sleep soundly at night, and learn to laugh again. He could even apologize to his fans in a few days. Or go Live right now and call it all off. Tell them to go home and lock their doors and bar their windows and crawl back to work on Monday telling their boss whatever lie would let them keep their jobs so they could just take their lives back.

But that wasn't going to happen, was it?

No one got off the hook anymore, no one forgave, no one forgot. Even presidents attacked private citizens, called them insulting names, lied about them.

Cro Magnons were extinct but this society was just as brutal. The savagery was subtler; lives were ruined these days by budget cuts and downsizing and salary caps and quarterly reports and absurd law changes and trolls and shaming and fake news. The one percent of the one percent of the one percent owned 90 percent of the wealth in the entire world and the rest attacked each other just to get the tiniest bit of what remained.

And in all honesty, none of that would touch Bob. He was one of the elite. He'd made obscene amounts of money. He could just enjoy what it bought him and his people.

No, he couldn't, not if he ever wanted to look himself in the eye again.

"D.C or bust," he said into his headset.

The pilot turned away from the other helicopter and flew towards the first hints of sunrise glowing along a distant horizon.

Chapter 64

"CIRCLE THE TRUCKS," THE main marine ordered. "Elders, get the children to the two finished homes, please! The rest are with us."

Lionel watched a horde of militia members and white supremacists thunder down on them, lowering their weapons now, taking aim at the people of the disappeared Hattiesburg.

"Oh hell no," he hollered.

A marine yelled at him, "You gonna get out of the way, Hollywood?"

Lionel turned, saw what he was standing in front of, and leaped for cover.

The soldiers were prepping three U.S. Military GAU 19B 50 Caliber Gatling guns they had liberated from the processing center's weapons storehouse.

"Aryans and rednecks and nazis, oh my," Lionel called, grinning at the mega weapons called Terrorist Killers.

And now he saw why; these guns were terrifying.

The marine hollered, "Ready!"

The guns swung from left to right—

"Aim!"

Each aimed at a slightly different area of the oncoming attackers—

"Fire!"

The modern Gatlings ripped the militias to shreds, dispensing most of the advancing forces within two horrifically efficient, deafening minutes.

Those still alive after that dreadful dose of hellfire fled back up the hill.

A sniper took them out one at a time.

The residents cheered.

Lionel signaled for quiet. "No partying yet," he called out, "we have more to do."

The marine agreed. "Grab guns. We'll teach you to use them quickly."

A young man asked, "Didn't we just win?"

Lionel clasped him on the shoulder. "Son, that was just the welcoming committee," he said. "The real numbers are definitely on their way, and they're gonna be really pissed."

Tears welled up in the young man's eyes. "Why?"

Lionel hugged him, speaking into his ear. "When did they ever let us win and walk away?" He pulled the would-be soldier so the kid stood before him. "If we want this, it ain't enough to take what's ours. We gotta show the whole twisted country we aim to keep it or die trying. Brace yourself, my brother, this ain't over by a damn sight."

The young man swallowed hard. "O-okay," he managed. "I ain't going backwards."

"Smartest thing anyone ever said in this country," Lionel exclaimed.

It startled the young man. His eyes widened until Lionel's meaning registered, and then the kid stood straighter, threw back his shoulders, raised his head, and broke into a smile that came from deep down in his soul. "We're in this, all the way."

"Damn straight."

Chapter 65

ALL PERMITS AND PAPERWORK had been filled out to perfection, so workers set up saw horses sectioning off the already gathering crowd at the National Mall. Other workers set up a podium and microphone at the bottom of the steps leading to the Lincoln Memorial.

Curiously, a matching podium and a multitude of microphones were also set up on the landing half way up those historic steps.

No explanation was provided.

People were allowed to gather in front of the lower podium, but no one was permitted onto the steps. A squad of police in riot gear made sure the Lincoln Memorial stayed off limits all morning.

Still, the crowd persisted in gathering....

Chapter 66

AMY BROOKS WAS REPORTING from another hotel room. She seemed a little less tense than her last broadcast, almost back on her game. "TASE continues to spread across the country, pursuing Bob Murphy and other alleged enemies of the state."

"But Bob Murphy isn't an enemy of the American people. Even today, his message went out seeking to unify Americans peacefully against the ongoing derailment of the 'Idea of America' as he said.

"There is truth in that, and value in unity, especially in the face of those who would oppress freedoms and subvert ideas—"

She was cut off by the booming crack of wood. Startled, Amy looked to her left, horror twisting her face—

The broadcast picked up the sound of running boots—

Amy raised an arm defensively —

A Stinger battering ram slammed into view, knocking her thin arm aside, plowing right into Amy Brooks' face.

Shattering her cheekbone.

Caving in her skull.

Black uniformed torsos filled the screen.

The ominous thud of heavy boots kicking where

Amy's body fell continued long after the sounds of gurgling and gasping stopped....

Chapter 67

AS THEY FLEW TOWARD DC, father and son did not speak. Instead, Bob stared at the cellphone picture of Mary Angeline's portrait he took before fleeing their home, and did what he had done throughout his career; he tried out his material on the one opinion he trusted above all others.

In his mind, he performed the whole speech for her, even adding in what he hoped the audience would say. When he was finished, he imagined an entire conversation with the love of his life.

And his heart warmed with the sense that she liked what he planned.

He winked at her smiling image and murmured, "See ya soon," before shutting down his phone.

Chapter 68

MORE CAME.

Militias from neighboring towns, and then across the county, and then, according to shoulder patches, the furthest reaches of the state. And yet, Hattiesburg residents were winning.

Some had paid the price. The old man who only wanted to read Walter Mosley took one right in the heart and died on the spot.

Grace Wilkins, who wanted to cook using her own kitchen, was shot through the eye.

Numerous others sustained wounds.

But mostly, they were winning enough to think the U.S. military had to arrive soon and put an end to the madness.

That had to happen, right?

And then more Aryans crested the ridge. So many they blurred the horizon.

Two women fainted.

Most of the rest looked exhausted, scared, their faith faltering.

And then they heard the jets. Still in the distance, but visible now.

The military was at long last swooping down from the skies to save the day, to end the horror, to, in the eleventh hour, bring them some peace.

"That's right, run," Lionel murmured, delighted to watch a hill full of whiteboys retreat as one. He took in all of devastated Hattiesburg. Death everywhere. Blood everywhere else.

Shadows crossed the sky.

Lionel looked up, his heart swelling to see those fighter planes.

"Finally, the cavalry arri—"

Hope died in his chest as the bombs began dropping overhead....

Chapter 69

BOB AND JACKSON'S PILOT took the 'copter right down into the rally, landing on a space kept clear for their arrival on the great lawn near the Lincoln Memorial. Police provided an escort, a lieutenant promising Bob, "We'll be waiting right offstage when you are done. Everything is going to go smoothly."

Bob wasn't sure whom it was going to go smoothly for, but he climbed the steps to the podium anyway.

Jackson's phone vibrated and he gave it a glance. There was a picture of Dolores hugging an ecstatic Perri and an awkwardly accepting Merle on their private plane. Bodyguards filled the space all around them.

"Thank God," Jackson sighed, looking up to show his father, but it was too late; Bob Murphy had already stepped onstage.

There were people as far as the comedian's eye could see, sectioned off in squares on either side of the reflecting pool, all the way back to the Washington Monument. Soldiers lined the walkways between the sectioned-off crowds, but the millions and millions didn't seem to mind.

Their voice was overpowering.

"BOB! BOB! BOB! BOB!"

It took him several minutes to quiet them enough to speak.

"It's been a really long time since I've seen you, really really seen you," he said. "And by God, you are so beautiful!"

The crowd roared its love right back to him. When he could be heard again, he put off his planned speech, just wanting to speak with the astounding mass of like-minded people. "After Mary Angeline passed, I was lost, and I .... I was breathing, and meant well, but I wasn't really living.

"Living means more than obsessing on our own personal dramas. We humans, we silly, vulnerable humans, we're a community, and with community comes a responsibility to get involved, to help, to contribute, to add to the forward progress we all make.

"That's what it means to be alive ... really alive, and I am so grateful to each and every one of you, and to my son, Jackson, and to my Mary Angeline because right now I can honestly say, for the first time in a really long while, I am so freaking alive!"

The cheers washed over him in waves.

He held up a hand, spoke again. "We are a simple gathering, covered by the Constitution, supported by the dreams of our Founding Fathers, the guys who designed this whole crazy experiment."

Applause and cheers drowned him out for a minute.

"You know, Jefferson and Franklin and Adams and all those other imperfect maniacs, they wanted us to have a say in how things worked around here.

"For too long, that is not the way it has been.

"But we still have those rights. We still have that voice.

"And today we're going to use it."

The cheers made him wait a full minute.

"That's what we're gonna do together. We're all

going to say our piece now, hands up so no one gets the idea that we are dangerous."

An ocean of hands went up. So did more roaring cheers.

The soldiers seemed shocked by the sheer power of the unified action. Some raised their weapons just a bit closer to their chests.

"Let's hold hands together so they really know we have no weapons besides our voice and our votes."

Millions of people joined hands.

Behind him and to the right, Bob saw members of Congress forming at the other podium. He suspected his microphone would be cut off in a moment.

"Hey fellas," he waved to them, inspiring gentle laughter from millions, who he returned his attention to. "We've got some guests up there so let's just tell them."

The crowd roared its approval. Bob comically pretended to struggle with the podium as he repositioned it so he could face the elected officials or the crowd with just a slight movement.
The crowd laughed at his physical comedy, applauded his success.

The elected officials seemed stunned by Bob's easy command over so many.

"Congressmen, we're going to make a simple request based on the suggestions of these fine Americans you see here. I'm gonna read our suggestions —wait, make that demands— and we're going to give you one week to put them into law. If you can't listen to We, The People, if you can't serve us like you've been elected to do, we'd like President Statler and every member of Congress to retire at the end of their current terms. If you can't give us the more perfect union we want, then you have failed America, and you are fired."

An ocean of joined hands shot up over millions of heads and shook in unison. An incredibly loud cheer shook Bob's spine.

And then he heard it.

Amid all that cheering.

A laugh.

Just one laugh.

The Laugh.

"Mary Angeline," Bob murmured.

Bob couldn't hear himself over the roaring crowd. In fact, the cheers were so deafening no one heard the shot.

Bob Murphy fell, dead before he hit the ground.

For almost a minute nothing happened. The crowd's faces devolved from elation to shock, from realization to horror ... and then to steely determination.

Four people raised their joined hands. Others did likewise until the mall was a sea of unity.

The soldiers were prepared for enemy combatants, not for Americans, real unarmed Americans, arms raised, hands devoid of weapons, their bodies seeming to indicate surrender but their faces ... their faces promising something else entirely.

Corporal Wilson, always a bit jumpy, shot first.

The rest followed.

It didn't matter.

The crowd surged forward, and the military had nowhere near enough bullets for all of them....

AUTHOR'S NOTE

THIS BOOK IS DEDICATED to my late father, Bernard Patrick Francis Ryan. He was an old school Conservative who taught me about the strength of believing in the Idea of America, and who would want to give today's politicians a swift kick in the ass.

This book is written for my sons, Sean and Tyler, and all of my students past, present, and future, because I want them to know the old man spoke up when speaking up was needed.

This book exists because every day the goddess Tina gives me the strength to try.

Silvio, my intimidating managing editor, gets no praise whatsoever. Do not believe him if he tries to tell you otherwise.

My body and health plan thank friends and family who didn't punch me when I spoke way too often and at length about wanting to write this for years and years.

My deepest thanks goes to my trusted and beloved first content approvers ("Is it a story? Huh? Huh? Is it?") and proofreaders, the goddess Tina and the legendary Cindi Ortiz.

Special thanks goes to a group who agreed to read an unpolished draft to give feedback and, in some cases, crucial editorial guidance. These incredibly generous and insightful souls are Michael Rogers, Caseen Gaines,

Roger Ross, Maria Perry, Imogene Papp, Elizabeth Walker, Alex Simmons, and Jean-Michael Akey. Special added thanks to Roger for remembering and allowing me to use "Well Fed Sons" which he wrote when we were wee lads. Additional thanks to 107.1 The Peak, and, when I really needed a boost, David Johansen. Lastly, special thanks to Stephen King, whose *Mr. Mercedes*, *Finders Keepers*, and *End of Watch* kept me energized to write.

An American wrote this novella for all Americans. It is not meant to be used in service of any political party. However, all patriotic souls are welcome to embrace the Idea of America expressed within and work toward a more perfect union together.

OTHER WORK BY THE AUTHOR:

~*FICTION*~

THE MALLORY AND GUNNER SERIES:
Ciy Of Sin
City Of Woe
City Of Pain
City Of Love (coming soon)

THE UNWANTED SERIES:
Genius High (coming soon)
Perfect
The Unwanted

~*ALEX SIMMONS' BLACKJACK*~

Blackjack Shooters
Ransom For A Dead King
Driven
Dark End Of The Rainbow (Coming Soon)
Trial By Fire/Trial By Ice

~*CHILDREN'S FICTION*~

THE FERGUSON FILES:
The Mystery Spot (coming soon)
The Dance Dilemma
The Beach House Burglaries

~*FILM*~

(available through Feenix Films)
Lock-Load-Love
(co-writer, assistant producer, actor)
Nicky Newark (actor)
Clandestine (associate producer, actor)

FROM SEAMUS AND NUNZIO PRODUCTION
(coming soon)
Zombies Of New Milford
(writer, director, producer, lyrics, actor)

~*SHORT FILMS*~

For Amanda Kaminsky
"In Too Deep" (actor)

For Michael Errichiello
"Presumed Strangers" (actor)

~*PODCASTS*~

Tell The Damn Story

OUR FOUNDERS

Made in the USA
Middletown, DE
23 December 2017